BATTERED AND BURIED

AN ALL-DAY BREAKFAST CAFÉ MYSTERY

Battered and Buried

Lena Gregory

THORNDIKE PRESS
A part of Gale, a Cengage Company

GALE
A Cengage Company

Thorndike Press® Large Print Softcover Cozy Mystery.
The text of this Large Print edition is unabridged.
Other aspects of the book may vary from the original edition.
Set in 16 pt. Plantin.

LIBRARY OF CONGRESS CIP DATA ON FILE.
CATALOGUING IN PUBLICATION FOR THIS BOOK
IS AVAILABLE FROM THE LIBRARY OF CONGRESS.

ISBN-13: 978-1-4205-1851-1 (softcover alk. paper)

Published in 2024 by arrangement with Beyond the Page Publishing, LLC.

Printed in the USA
1 2 3 4 5   28 27 26 25 24

CAST OF CHARACTERS

Gia Morelli — Owner, All-Day Breakfast Café

Thor — Gia's Bernese mountain dog

Klondike — Gia's black and white kitten

Savannah Mills — Gia's best friend, former real estate agent

Pepper — Savannah's gray and white tabby kitten

Captain Hunter Quinn (Hunt) — Gia's fiancé, Savannah's cousin, captain of the Boggy Creek PD

Leo Dumont — Savannah's fiancé, Hunt's partner

Harley Anderson — homeless man

Earl Dennison — Older man, Gia's first ever customer at the All-Day Breakfast Café

Cole Barrister — Retired, full-time cook at All-Day Breakfast Café

Cybil Devane — Mysterious older woman who often walks in the woods

Alfie Todd — Freelance information analyst

Trevor Barnes — Owner of Storm Scoopers, ice cream parlor on Main Street

Brandy — Trevor's German shepherd

Zeus and Ares — Trevor's guard dogs, Akitas

Willow Broussard — All-Day Breakfast Café's full-time waitress

Skyla Broussard — Willow's mother

Zoe — Owner of the Doggie Daycare Center

Donna Mae Parker — Harley's ex-girlfriend, flower shop owner

Joey Mills — Savannah's youngest brother

Michael Mills — Savannah's brother, works in construction

James, Luke, and Ben Mills — Savannah's other brothers

CHAPTER ONE

Already an hour late for work, thanks to the mess left by an overeager raccoon who'd gotten into her garbage pails — again — despite the two hundred dollars she'd spent on supposedly raccoon-proof bins, Gia Morelli hit her car's lock button, dropped the key fob into her bag, and hurried in through the back door of the bustling All-Day Breakfast Café. She inhaled deeply the scent of bacon and freshly baked blueberry muffins, counted to three, then eased the breath out. She'd have to figure out what to do about the raccoon, unless she wanted to continue to pick up garbage as part of her morning routine, but now wasn't the time to worry about it.

"Gia, hey, how's it going?" Savannah Mills, her best friend and one of her waitresses, rushed past her and into the kitchen without pausing for an answer. Using the back of her wrist, she shoved back a few strands of long blonde hair that had come free from her braid as she added a ticket to the line already hanging above the grill.

Gia followed. She checked the clock above the cutout between the kitchen and dining room. Almost noon on a Sunday. Churches had just let out, ballgames were over or about to begin, and many local businesses were closed. Her gaze shifted through the cutout to the packed dining room. Every table was full, as were all the counter stools. A shiver raced through her, raising goose bumps.

She'd finally realized her dream — a thriving café where people gathered to enjoy good food, a cozy atmosphere, and stoke the Boggy Creek rumor mill. All in all, her life had become a success, a far cry from the bottom she'd hit before leaving her old life in New York City behind. How had she ever missed that life? Ever contemplated going back? She had no idea, but now . . . Well, now she'd better get her act together and pitch in.

Shaking off any lingering thoughts of her past, she donned an apron, washed her hands, and grabbed a pair of gloves. She'd already tied her long, wavy brown hair back before leaving the house. "What do you need, Cole?"

Cole Barrister, her good friend and full-time cook since he'd come to realize retirement didn't suit him, scanned the line of tickets. "Wanna do the breads and potatoes?"

"You've got it." The two of them fell into their usual easy rhythm as Cole worked the grill and Gia toasted breads and bagels and plated breakfast potatoes.

He spared her a quick glance, his eyes lit with humor. "Lemme guess — the raccoon again?"

"Yup. And I don't want to talk about it."

He chuckled to himself. "I guess the new pails didn't work out so well?"

"I doubt they even slowed him down. He chewed right through the bungees and helped himself." Which might not even have been so bad — she didn't want to see any critter go hungry — if it didn't mean she had to spend an hour cleaning up all the garbage he left scattered across her yard.

While she absolutely loved the rural development on the outskirts of the Ocala National Forest, the critters that came with it kind of put a damper on things. Although she was much better now than when she'd first moved in and the sight of a snake would send her running. A chill tore through her at the thought.

Cole grinned, slid a long spatula beneath three eggs, and flipped them without breaking a yolk. "You gonna call someone now?"

She sighed, semi-resigned to the fact that she was going to have to hire someone to humanely relocate the little varmint. "We'll see."

He snickered as he slid the eggs onto a pile of hash.

Gia did what she always did when she wanted to procrastinate, changed the subject. "Any plans for tomorrow?"

Cole shrugged, his attention riveted on the multiple orders currently sizzling on the grill. "I'm not sure yet. How about you?"

"I'm thinking of taking the day to go kayaking with Trevor." An activity she'd surprisingly come to enjoy, though she'd always loved spending time with her good friend Trevor Barnes, who owned Storm Scoopers — the ice cream parlor down Main Street from the café.

"Hunt working?" Cole asked.

Her fiancé — she rolled the term around in her head for a moment. Nope, it still felt foreign, even five months after he'd asked her to marry him — Detective Hunter Quinn would have joined them if he wasn't on duty. "Yeah, he and Leo both have to work, and Savannah's spending the day with her dad."

"Glad to hear it. How's her dad doing?" He piled bacon and eggs onto rolls Gia had already cut open, added salt, pepper, and ketchup to, and set on plates.

"He's doing well." Though Savannah and her father had always been close, he'd finally started getting out and about a little after becoming somewhat of a recluse following his wife's death more than twenty years ago. "I think almost losing Savannah encouraged him to spend more time with her out of the house."

Cole shook his head, the memory of Savannah's kidnapping no doubt haunting him as it did all of them.

Though, at least some good had come from the harrowing experience. In addition to spending more time with her father, Savannah had also come to work at the café, giving her and Gia more time together as well, especially now that she'd gotten married and moved out of Gia's spare bedroom and into her own house. Granted, Savannah's house was right down the road from Gia's, but still . . .

The kitchen door opened and Savannah poked her head in. "Gia?"

"Yeah?"

"I'm sorry to bother you, but . . ." Tears

11

shimmered in her big blue eyes as Savannah caught her lower lip between her teeth and glanced through the cutout toward the dining room. Despite her diminutive build and easygoing manner, Savannah was one of the strongest women Gia knew, and she was more than capable of handling even the rowdiest customers. Something had to be really wrong for her to be so upset. "Could you come out front for a minute? We have a . . . uh . . . situation."

Cole paused, spatula held poised above the grill. "You need me to come out?"

"No, no," she answered quickly. Too quickly.

"You okay here for a minute, Cole?" Though she knew he'd be fine no matter how busy they got.

"Sure."

She ripped off her gloves, dropped them into the trash can, and followed Savannah out into the hallway. As soon as they were out of earshot, she whispered, "What's going on?"

Savannah blew out a breath, ruffling the few wisps of blonde hair that had come loose from her braid. "Some guy out there's got me madder than a wet hen. He's putting up a stink, and he insists on speaking to the owner, despite me doin' everything under the sun to please his highfalutin —"

"Okay." Better to stop the rant before she got worked up any further. "What's his problem?"

"I don't know exactly." Savannah flung her arms to the sides, her gaze skittering to the closed doors that led to the dining room. "Everything, it seems. He's been giving us a hard time since he walked in the door. I almost asked him to leave, but, well, you know I hate to lose business or do anything to cause a scene."

"Who waited on him?" Though whether it was Savannah or Willow made no difference, as they were both not only competent but friendly too.

"I did."

Gia would have shrugged it off if not for how upset Savannah was. But she'd deal with it. It wouldn't be the first time a customer had been unhappy with something, though, thankfully, it didn't happen often. She'd simply fix whatever was bothering him and that would be that. Hopefully, he wouldn't cause too much trouble. The last thing she needed was another stint on the gossip mill.

Her hopes were dashed, however, when she pushed through the swinging doors into the dining room and noted an agitated

13

customer stalking back and forth along the counter and the Bailey twins, Estelle and Esmeralda, Boggy Creek's very own gossip-mongers, seated smack in his path.

She should have just stayed in bed this morning. Shaking off her growing unease, she plastered on a smile and held out a hand as she intercepted him. "Hi, I'm Gia Morelli. It's a pleasure to meet you."

Ignoring her hand, he propped his hands on his hips. "You own this dive?"

Irked, Gia lowered her hand to her side and resisted the urge to squirm beneath his hostile stare. She bit the inside of her cheek to cage the tirade that begged to escape. "I'm the owner. How can I help you?"

He wore a gray business suit, the top button of his lavender shirt open, his pin-striped tie loosened, perhaps in deference to the Florida heat, and a thick gold ring circled his right pinky. He wore his closely cropped dark hair ruthlessly slicked back. It was his eyes that drew her attention, though. Cold, dark gray eyes that brought to mind the winter skies she'd left behind in New York. "You want to help me?"

She waited him out.

A woman stood, arms folded, watching him. Sun-streaked strawberry blonde hair hung in waves, framing delicate features and catlike green eyes — eyes that tracked his every movement. Despite the spectacle the guy was causing, and the fact that her attention was riveted on him, she didn't appear concerned, or even surprised. If anything, she seemed bored by his outburst. If she was his companion, which Gia couldn't ask Savannah at the moment, she would guess the woman had witnessed this behavior before.

"Fine. If you want to do something for me . . ." The guy pointed a finger at Gia, no more than an inch from her face, whipping her attention back to him. "Close up and go back to New York."

She gasped before she could catch herself. Concerned by his aggression, she scanned the café just as her other waitress, Willow Broussard, slipped through the swinging doors into the back hallway.

Savannah stood behind the counter talking quietly on the phone. The fact that Gia had a strict "no cell phones on the floor" policy assured her she was most likely summoning help.

Skyla Broussard, Willow's mother and Gia's counterperson, stood frozen beside the register, bag held out toward Donna Mae Parker, who made no move to take it from her.

Gia didn't dare shift her gaze to the Bailey twins, who were no doubt salivating at the spectacle.

"Other than that, you can't do anything for me." The guy leaned closer.

Gia held her ground. No way was she backing up and giving him so much as an inch.

"I don't know who you have running your grill back there, but whoever it is has no clue what he's doing."

She bristled. She'd received tons of five-star Google reviews, many of which referenced Cole's cooking as well as some of his original recipes. Still . . . she had to maintain some semblance of control with the entire packed dining room hanging on her every word. Or, at least, her irate customer's every word. It was time to deescalate the situation. "Look, sir —"

"The eggs were rubbery, the toast soggy, and the breakfast potatoes greasy."

"I'm sorry you —"

"And don't even get me started on the service."

"Look, buddy." She raised her voice so he couldn't steamroll over her again. "I'm sorry you weren't happy with your meal. There will be no charge for today, and I can offer you a gift certificate if you'd like —"

"Gift certificate?" He scoffed. "You couldn't pay me to eat in this dump again."

"That's fine, sir." And now she'd had just about enough. This guy had come into her establishment, trashed the food, insulted her employees, and made all of her customers uncomfortable — probably with the exception of the Bailey sisters. No wonder Savannah was so upset. Seemed to Gia this guy had come in for the sole purpose of causing trouble. "If there's nothing more I can do for you, then I'm afraid I'll have to ask you to leave."

He lifted a brow and stared her down. As his gaze slid past her, the corner of his mouth twitched up in a smirk.

"Is there a problem here?" Cole lay a hand on her shoulder, angled himself in front of Gia, and came face-to-face with the guy. His face went pale. "Bragge?"

The guy — Bragge? — only grinned. "Cole Barrister. Why am I not surprised? You never could run a proper kitchen. Or a proper household, if I remember correctly."

Cole fisted one hand.

Whoa. Gia stepped between them before he could use it. "Okay, this has gone far enough."

But Cole's gaze had moved past Bragge to the woman standing behind him, her shoul-

17

der resting against the doorway, folded arms lifting her ample cleavage, and he froze.

Savannah appeared at Gia's side and leveled Bragge with a scathing glare. "Sir, I believe you've been asked to leave, and since the police are on their way, I suggest you do so. Immediately."

Bragge eyeballed Gia, then Savannah, and dismissed them to turn his glare on Cole. "You might want to start looking for a new job, old pal, because I don't think this place is going to last long."

Cole continued to stare at the woman, jaw clenched tight enough to shatter teeth.

Gia opened her mouth to say something, then snapped it closed just as quickly when Bragge whirled on one heel and strode toward the door. As he reached it, the door opened.

Trevor walked in, narrowed his gaze at Bragge, then held the door as the guy stormed out with the woman on his heels. When he reached Gia, he hooked a thumb over his shoulder. "What was he doing here?"

Tremors racked Gia's entire body as the adrenaline rush subsided. She loathed conflict, and the experience had left her shaky and slightly scared — not of Bragge, but of how Cole had reacted to him. She

18

tried for a smile. "I g-guess he didn't like his breakfast."

"Huh." Trevor looked in the direction Bragge had gone then back at Gia. His gaze skipped to Savannah then Cole, and he frowned. "I might be mistaken, but I'm pretty sure that's the guy who rented out the space across the street from me where Hank's Hardware used to be when Hank moved over to Bayshore Lane. That's what I was just coming to tell you . . . uh . . ."

"Trevor?" Gia barely resisted the urge to snap her fingers to regain his attention.

He paused, looked around the dining room, and turned beet red. "Uh . . . You know what? I was just coming in for breakfast. Could you do a to-go order?"

"Um, yeah, sure." She tried to regain her equilibrium as she took hold of Cole's elbow and led him and Trevor back toward the kitchen while Savannah, Willow, and Skyla worked to reassure customers and regain some semblance of control in the dining room.

The instant the doors swung shut behind her, Gia whirled on both of them. "What was that all about? Who was that guy?"

"Sorry, Gia." Trevor's short brown hair hung long in the front, and he shook it back out of his eyes. "I caught myself when I realized I was about to announce your new competition in front of a roomful of customers."

"Competition?" What was he talking about? She'd heard Hank had moved out of the building down the road to somewhere bigger, thanks to record growth in the area, but she hadn't yet heard what was going to replace the hardware store.

"Yeah. He's opening a deli with indoor and outdoor seating." When his hair flopped back into his face, Trevor raked it back with his hand. "And he plans to serve breakfast all day."

Her heart sank. Was it possible her dream would be this short-lived? Surely, the clientele she'd built would remain loyal. Wouldn't they? She whirled on Cole, who'd remained uncharacteristically quiet throughout the entire incident. "Cole? Want to tell me what the deal is? How do you know that guy?"

His usually ruddy complexion remained pallid as he met her gaze and sighed. "That, my dear, is going to be a problem."

CHAPTER TWO

It took more than two hours to catch up after falling behind, as well as serve all the new customers who streamed into the café as news of the confrontation spread. Huh. Seemed Rusty Bragge's efforts to sabotage her had had the opposite effect. At least in the short term. Who knew what the long-term effects would be? If people remembered the scene he'd caused, maybe they'd recognize it for what it was — an effort to put her down so he could then build himself up. Of course, Gia's experience in Boggy Creek had taught her some rumors faded quickly, and people forgot as life moved on. She'd also learned the residents of Boggy Creek were nothing if not loyal. She'd have to keep that in mind.

Since she'd already filed a complaint with her fiancé, Captain Hunter Quinn, and Savannah's husband, Detective Leo Dumont, and Cole had remained tight-lipped about the entire incident, there wasn't much else she could do. Although the man had disappeared before the police had arrived, they'd promised to have a talk with him when they could track him down.

Gia sighed and stripped off her gloves, then checked through the cutout to the dining room. Only three tables contained customers, and all of them had been served. She checked the clock. They should have about an hour before business picked up again. Leaving the stack of pots she'd just finished washing to put away later, she turned to Cole.

He must have felt her gaze land on him, because he stiffened, even with his back to her, as he continued to clean the grill.

She leaned back against the center island, folded her arms, and waited him out.

It only took a few minutes for him to pause and turn to her. He tossed the brush he'd been using into the sink she'd just emptied and his gloves in the garbage pail. "What?"

She lifted a brow. She'd already decided she wouldn't question him. She'd tried that, and all it had gotten her was two hours of the silent treatment. So, she'd wait him out, and when he was ready, hopefully he'd tell her what was going on. Because he wasn't acting like himself at all.

"All right, fine. I'm sorry." He shook his head and shoved a hand through shaggy salt-and-pepper hair that hung just past the collar of his Hawaiian print shirt. "Rusty Bragge is a sore subject for me. Unfortunately, he's about the closest I've ever come to having a nemesis."

"Hey." Not that she knew a lot about his life before he retired and moved to Rolling Pines, the development he and Gia both lived in, but she couldn't imagine the kind, soft-spoken man she knew having enemies. She waited for him to look up at her, then moved closer and took his hand in hers. "You have nothing to be sorry for, Cole. You haven't done anything wrong, and I understand if you needed a little space. There's no need to apologize for that, or for anything else. I'm just worried about you."

His jaw clenched, and he nodded.

The kitchen door swung open, and Savannah strode through carrying two mugs. "It just slowed down out there, so I thought you guys might want coffee."

"Thanks, Savannah." Though the last thing she probably needed with her nerves still jittery was caffeine.

After setting the mugs on the island, she turned toward Gia and Cole, who were still standing together by the grill. "Oh, gosh, I'm sorry. I didn't mean to interrupt."

"That's okay. If Willow and Skyla can handle the front, you may as well sit with us. That way, we only have to go through this once." Cole squeezed Gia's hand before releasing her and pulling two stools out. He gestured for Gia and Savannah to sit, then rounded the island and sat on a stool across from them.

"O-kay." Savannah glanced at Gia, but Gia could only shrug as they both took their seats.

Cole slid his coffee in front of him, then turned the mug a few times without taking a sip. "First let me tell you what kind of man Rusty Bragge is. Because that's the easier part to tell."

Gia only nodded, afraid he'd clam up if she said the wrong thing.

"Rusty is probably the most crooked, least successful weasel I've ever had the misfortune to know." He released the mug and clenched his fists on the countertop. "He makes a habit of finding a business that works, then publicly trashing the place, leaving a slew of bogus bad reviews, and beating the owners down until they either give up and close or lose too much business to remain open, all while opening his own

24

business in direct competition with his victim's."

"You don't have to worry about that, Cole." Gia reached across the counter and lay a hand over his fist. "I'm not going anywhere."

"You say that now, but you don't know what it's like." He plastered his hands against the counter, then shoved to his feet. His stool rocked precariously, balanced on two legs for a moment, then managed to remain upright as Cole began to pace. "He's vicious, Gia. He's mean, he's spiteful, and he'll stop at nothing to get his way."

Gia's mind stuck on *spiteful.* Of what little Cole had said so far, that was the one word that stuck out, because to her, spiteful implied personal. And since she had never met the man before now, he couldn't possibly have any kind of grudge toward her. But what had Cole said earlier? Rusty was the closest he'd ever come to having a nemesis. And that seemed personal.

"After he sets his sights on someone, he destroys them. And you wanna know the worst part about it? The businesses he opens are never successful. They always fail, and he files bankruptcy and moves on to his next mark."

"I don't understand." She resisted the

25

urge to step in front of him or tell him to sit as he continued to stalk back and forth across the kitchen. "How does he make a living if all of his businesses fail?"

"He doesn't." He stopped then, looked her dead in the eye. His face turned beet red. "His wife makes a good living. And she supports him."

Uh-oh. She had a feeling she'd just stumbled into the personal part as she remembered the stunning woman who'd stood beside the door while Rusty had gone on his tirade . . . and Cole's reaction to seeing her. "Was that the woman who was with him?"

"Yeah. Amanda."

"You know her?"

He plopped onto the stool, shoulders slumped, and Gia wished he'd go back to pacing again. At least then he hadn't seemed so defeated. "I thought I did."

He propped his elbows on the counter and rubbed his eyes, then raked his fingers through his hair and left them there, cradling his head in one hand.

Gia stood and went to him, resting a hand on his back.

Savannah, who'd remained quiet until then, grabbed a water bottle from the refrigerator and held it out to him. "Here,

26

honey, take a drink. You know you don't have to tell us anything you don't want to talk about, right?"

He shrugged and uncapped the water.

"But we're here if you do want to talk." She smiled. Savannah had the kind of smile that encouraged trust.

Gia squeezed Cole's shoulder, then returned to her seat and gestured for Savannah to do the same. Cole had needed space earlier, and she had a feeling he did again. He'd have to tell his story in his own time, in his own way. After he dealt with whatever memories haunted him.

She did know one thing, though. Rusty Bragge would not get away with taking the All-Day Breakfast Café away from her. She'd worked too hard, been through too much, to allow anyone to interfere with her dream. And he would definitely not get away with hurting Cole. She'd take him down for that alone.

"Look, guys. I really appreciate you both." Cole stood. "And I will explain everything, I promise, but for right now, would you mind if I took the rest of the afternoon off? I'm sorry to leave you stuck if it's going to get busy later, especially after . . . well . . . you know . . ."

"No problem, Cole. We'll be fine. Are you

sure you're okay, though?" She wasn't sure being alone was the best thing for him at the moment.

"Yeah. I'll be okay. What happened between . . ." He swallowed hard. "Rusty and me was a long time ago. It doesn't matter anymore. It hasn't for a long time."

"Sometimes old wounds run the deepest," Gia said softly.

"That ain't no lie." He walked out then, leaving Gia and Savannah looking after him.

"What are you doing to do?" Savannah stood and took both still-full mugs to the sink.

"I don't know yet, but I do know Rusty isn't going to get away with this. Not this time." Not if she could help it. "Would you be all right to work the grill if anyone comes in?"

"Sure thing." She frowned. "Where are you going?"

Gia yanked off her apron and hung it on the hook beside the door. "To have a chat with Rusty Bragge."

"Do you think that's a good idea?" Savannah hurried after her as she strode into the hallway. "Hunt and Leo said they'd talk to him. Maybe you should just wait."

"I'm not waiting." She grabbed her purse and keys from her office across the hall. She was done letting anyone else dictate the course of her life. She'd made that mistake with her ex-husband and what had that gotten her? Years dragged through criminal court and divorce court. It had almost destroyed her. Well, no thank you. She'd left that weak, vulnerable woman behind in New York. No way would Rusty Bragge get away with doing this to her.

Savannah gestured toward her bag. "Where exactly are you going to look for him?"

"At the shop he's renting." At least, that's where she'd start.

"And you're driving?" She quirked a brow.

"Oh." The shop was only right down Main Street. It would probably take her longer to find a parking spot than it would to walk the short distance. She grinned at Savannah, then dropped the keys into her bag and returned it to the desk drawer. "You're right."

"I know I am," she said and grinned back, "or I wouldn't have said it."

Gia smoothed the pink tunic top she wore over black leggings and took a deep breath. She counted to ten, breathing in and out slowly, until she regained her composure.

"Better?"

"Yup." She hugged Savannah then stepped

back. "Thank you, but I'm okay now."

She nodded.

"I'm just going to take a walk down there and peek in the windows, see if they've started renovations yet, get an idea how much time I might have to come up with a plan."

"A plan to do what exactly?" She folded her arms and leaned a shoulder against the doorjamb.

"A plan to save the business I worked so hard for." For a moment, an image of the woman — Amanda, according to Cole — in a similar pose as she'd waited for her husband to finish his rant flashed before her. Maybe Rusty wasn't the one she should be looking for. Perhaps she'd get further with Amanda. She shook off the thought. It seemed like a betrayal to Cole to seek out Amanda without first giving him the opportunity to explain what had happened between them.

Savannah opened her mouth as if to speak, then caught her bottom lip between her teeth and swallowed whatever argument she'd been contemplating. "Just promise me you won't get into another altercation with that man."

"Sure thing." If nothing else, the walk would probably help calm her nerves.

"Besides, it's Sunday, so he's probably not even there anyway."

Savannah nodded but didn't look convinced.

Figuring it was as close as she was apt to get to approval, Gia hugged her again, then hurried through the café with a quick check to be sure everything was running smoothly and out the front door. The heat sucker punched her the instant she stepped onto the walkway, and she paused as the warmth seeped into her, easing the tension from her muscles. She rolled her shoulders, tilted her head back and forth, then lifted her face to the sun.

What was she doing? What purpose would another confrontation with Rusty serve? She started walking toward what was once a hardware store, no competition to her whatsoever, then jumped and turned at the sound of her name.

Harley Anderson, a homeless man who'd become not only a good friend to Gia but somewhat of a guardian angel to both her and Savannah, strode across Main Street toward her. Somehow, he always seemed to show up just when she needed help. "You okay?"

"I am, thank you, Harley. How are you?"

Not much on small talk, Harley ignored

the question. "He shouldn't have talked to you like that."

It took her a moment to connect the dots. Donna Mae, who'd dated Harley once upon a time and had recently reconnected with him, must have told him about the confrontation. "No, he shouldn't have."

"I'm sorry I wasn't there." Thanks to a past trauma, Harley was unable to stand being indoors. Just the thought of going into an enclosed space, even a house or store, even for a single moment, brought him unbearable anxiety.

"Hey, it's no problem. It wasn't even that big a deal." The sudden realization that what she'd told Harley was actually true leeched out any remaining anger, leaving her clearheaded for the first time since this morning.

"You know I'd have come inside to help you if I knew what was going on." He rocked back and forth, long hair swinging with him, hand pressed against his more gray than blonde beard.

"Hey, Harley. I'm serious. It's no big deal. I know you'd always come if I needed help. Just like you always have."

He nodded, not seeming fully convinced.

"Are you hungry?"

He shrugged. "I could eat."

"Come on." She hooked her arm through his elbow then walked with him around the side of the shop. Whatever confrontation she was doomed to have with Rusty Bragge could wait until another time. "I just realized I'm starved. Why don't we sit out back and have dinner together?"

He smiled. "I'd like that."

"Me too." She'd have dinner with Harley, then give Cole a call and make sure he was okay once she closed. Then tomorrow, she'd go kayaking with Trevor and set aside any thought of Rusty Bragge. Let the police deal with him. But if he came back into her place of business again, or bothered Cole in any way, the gloves were coming off.

CHAPTER THREE

Gia tilted her face up toward the scorching Florida sunshine and closed her eyes, determined to keep the prior day's fiasco from intruding on her peace and quiet. Allowing her kayak to drift for just a moment along the Ocklawaha River through the Ocala National Forest, she inhaled deeply, filling her lungs with the sweet scent of star jasmine cascading from the trees in a blanket of white and green. Springtime in Boggy Creek, Florida, brought gorgeous warm weather with less than usual humidity, very little rain, and . . . and an abundance of snakes she seemed to run across wherever she went. Her eyes shot open.

"It's perfect, isn't it?" Trevor grinned at her then gestured toward the forest. "I knew the first time I brought you here you'd be hooked."

She scooted up straighter when she noticed the monkeys skittering and tumbling among the mangroves and resumed the smooth strokes that kept her kayak alongside Trevor's. "You were right."

Hard to believe it was nearly summer again already. Time certainly flew when you were having fun. Careful to keep the kayak perfectly balanced, Gia pulled her cell phone from the pocket of her khaki shorts and snapped a few pictures of the monkeys playing. Thankfully, Trevor seemed to understand her desire to keep the day stress-free and had refrained from any further questions about Cole and the incident in the café.

"I remember a time when the sight of a gator would have had you hightailing it back to New York." Trevor pointed toward a large alligator sunning himself along the bank — probably waiting for one of the monkeys, or her, or Trevor to fall in.

But she remained silent and allowed Trevor to revel in his illusions (delusions, whatever) of her newfound bravery. Truthfully, the only reason she didn't immediately run for her life was fear of getting eaten. She figured it was probably safer to remain in the kayak and continue on her way, gliding through the sapphire water as smoothly and quietly as possible so as not to draw attention. But she kept a watchful eye on the beast, lest he decide he was hungry enough to tip her and have himself a snack.

"So, any wedding plans yet?" Though he'd asked casually enough, she had no doubt he was itching to jump into planning another wedding after he'd done such an amazing job on Savannah's when she'd finally married her sweetheart, Leo Dumont. "You know you and Hunt are welcome to have the wedding at my house."

House was an understatement. Mild-mannered, clumsy, adorable Trevor, as she'd found out quite some time after she'd met him, lived in a gorgeous mansion — which had rivaled Santa's castle and workshop when he'd decorated for Savannah and Leo's Christmas wedding. "Thank you, Trevor. I promise, as soon as I'm ready, you'll be the first to know. Then you and Savannah can go to town and plan the whole event."

"Seriously?" His eyes lit with glee.

Uh-oh. She may have just put her foot in her mouth. Now, she'd have to follow through, and she had no idea what the two of them might plan, but it was sure to be elaborate. She laughed. "As long as it's not too over-the-top."

"No problem." He continued to paddle smoothly through the water, his lean muscles straining beneath his short-sleeve T-shirt with each stroke. How someone who could barely walk without tripping over his own feet could manage to be so graceful when it came to outdoor activities was beyond her. He pointed toward the trees, where a group of the rhesus macaques she enjoyed so much swung and played. "Look."

"They always seem so happy and playful, don't they?"

"Sure do." He lay his paddle across the kayak and drifted. "I could watch them all day long."

"Me too." She cast a leery glance toward the bank behind her, where Godzilla continued to sunbathe, seemingly oblivious to their passing, then slowed to enjoy the show. She rolled her shoulders, which she knew would be sore tomorrow, but it was worth it to spend the day with Trevor enjoying the hobby she'd come to love most since moving to Florida.

A water moccasin sliced through the water beside her, a gentle reminder that no matter how beautiful or peaceful the forest might be, it was also deadly.

"Hey, how about an archway covered in star jasmine?"

She kept one eye glued to the snake. "Huh?"

"Jasmine. Over an arched trellis." He lifted his hands over his head and stretched them wide and then down, rocking his kayak.

She held her breath, prayed he wouldn't dump himself into the critter-infested river.

But he balanced himself before he could tip over.

The breath shot from her lungs, and she gripped the sides of her own kayak to keep it from rocking. "What are you talking about?"

"For your wedding." His grin shot straight to her heart. "If you think a year is long enough to wait, you could get married next May under a canopy of star jasmine in one of my gardens."

The image was breathtaking, but she and Hunt hadn't discussed wedding plans since he'd asked her to marry him. She glanced at the sun reflecting off the beautiful, heart-shaped diamond ring Captain Hunter Quinn had slid onto her left ring finger nearly five months ago. The thought of commitment had terrified her at one time.

She hadn't grown up with siblings or even cousins. Her mother had passed away when she was young, and her father had tossed her out the day she graduated high school. Then her ex-husband . . . She dismissed the thought. Her marriage to Bradley had ended in a nightmare, had almost cost her the life she'd fled New York to build when he'd been found dead in the dumpster behind her café. He had no business in this place of tranquility.

"Unless you'd rather a more traditional church wedding, with a reception at my place afterward."

Gia laughed. She couldn't help it. Trevor was nothing if not persistent. "I'll tell you what, Trevor, I haven't discussed any actual wedding plans with Hunt yet, but even if we decide to have the ceremony at the church, we'll do the reception at your house."

He pumped a fist and let out a "Whoop!," startling a few of the monkeys, who paused in their revelry to stare.

She didn't think Hunt would mind, though she probably should have discussed it with him first. If he was horribly opposed, she'd have to find a way to break it to Trevor, but watching the joy in his expression as he glanced around wondrously, she really hoped Hunt would agree. She crossed her fingers as she started to row again.

"This is going to be amazing. It's going to be the best wedding ever." He winked at her. "Except for Savannah's."

"That goes without saying." It didn't matter to her where she and Hunt got married. All that mattered was having her newfound family and friends surrounding her and Hunt when they said their I dos.

"Hey, look." Trevor pointed toward the far bank. "Isn't that Cole and Cybil?"

Gia squinted against the sun's glare. Seemed she wasn't the only one taking advantage of the gorgeous spring weather and the fact that she'd decided to close the café on Mondays to allow for more time spent with friends.

For a moment, happiness filled her, and she was grateful that Cole had been able to shake off the incident in the café the day before and head out with Cybil to enjoy the outdoors. Then she noted his posture.

He stood with his hands on his hips staring down at something. He raked a hand through his hair, shook his head, then looked over his shoulder.

His companion, and a good friend of Gia's, Cybil Devane, lay a hand on his shoulder. It was good to see Cybil had someone to walk with now. When Gia had first met the woman walking through the forest alone, she'd mistaken her for some kind of seer. While that theory had diminished as she'd gotten to know her better, Gia still couldn't deny Cybil's uncanny knack for reading people. Either way, she was just glad Cybil no longer spent her time wandering through the woods alone now that she and Cole had become close.

Angling her kayak toward the bank, Gia paddled closer.

Caesar, the beagle mix Cybil had adopted, cowered beside his owner's leg, whimpering.

A chill raced through Gia despite the intensity of the sun's rays. Something was wrong. "Trevor?"

"Yeah, something's going on." He lifted a hand to shield his eyes from the sun and yelled, "Hey, Cole."

Cole jumped and whirled toward them, flinging out an arm and stepping in front of Cybil as if to shield her from danger.

What in the world? Not that there wasn't plenty to fear in the swampy forest, but neither he nor Cybil had ever seemed afraid while hiking. "Are you guys okay?"

Though his stance relaxed, he still seemed agitated. "Can either of you get cell phone service?"

Gia checked her phone. Two bars. "I might have enough to get a call out."

"I've got nothing." Trevor reached the bank first, beached his kayak, and climbed out. He pulled it farther up the slippery incline then helped Gia out and moved her kayak as well.

She started toward Cole and Cybil. "Who do you need to call?"

"Nine-one-one." Cole held up a hand to stop them. "You may want to wait there."

The memory of the giant gator sunning himself had her stopping dead in her tracks. She held the phone out to him. "What is it? Is something wrong?"

Cole took the phone from her and stepped away to make the call.

Cybil remained with Gia and Trevor. Paleness tinged her usually tanned complexion.

When Gia glanced at Trevor, he simply shrugged and stuffed his hands into his pockets. He continued to scan the woods, with his gaze jumping back to Cole every couple of seconds.

Satisfied Trevor would keep an eye on Cole, Gia turned to Cybil. A quick study assured her Cybil seemed mostly okay. Physically, at least, though her hands shook as she lifted her long black hair streaked with white off her neck and fanned herself. Not once since she'd met her could Gia remember noticing her having any trouble with the excessive Florida heat. "You okay? Did one of you get hurt?"

"N-no, no. We're fine." She glanced at

Cole then scooped Caesar up into her arms and snuggled him against her. "But we f-found . . ."

"Calm down, Cybil. Take a few deep breaths." Gia had come across all sorts of wildlife while kayaking with Trevor and walking the well-marked trails with her Bernese mountain dog, Thor. She'd even once stumbled over a bod . . . oh, no. She grabbed Cybil's wrist. "What is it?"

Silently, she pointed over her shoulder.

"Wait here." Without waiting for her to agree, Gia started slowly in the direction Cybil had indicated, carefully scanning before each step to be sure nothing danger-ous lurked beneath the sea of ferns. Al-though, the ticks she dreaded were too small to notice. She'd have to check herself thoroughly the instant she got home.

She approached a gnarled jumble of roots, tiptoeing gingerly through the underbrush lest a snake lie in wait. Fear gripped her, and she barely resisted the urge to high-step her way back out of there, might even have done so if not for the arm clad in a light blue, long-sleeve Henley protruding from beneath the tangled vines. She sucked in a breath of the cloying scent of decay that permeated the swampy forest and stumbled back. Why would someone be out in the woods, despite the early summer heat, wearing long sleeves?

Really, Gia? There's a person lying in the brush, and that's what catches your attention — his fashion choices? Who knew? Maybe that bit of contradiction was easier for her mind to process than the truth of what she was seeing. When she backed into something solid, she jumped and plastered a hand against her chest to keep her heart caged there.

"Hey, it's just me." Cole lifted his hands in the air and backed up, then held out her cell phone.

"Did anyone check for a pulse?"

"I did, yes. He's beyond help."

She forced herself to breathe as she took the phone from him. "Did you get the police?"

"Yeah." He nodded and swiped a hand over his mouth. "They're on their way."

"Okay, good. That's good."

"But I don't know what I'm supposed to say to them when they get here." Cole stuffed both hands into his hair and squeezed the strands.

"It's okay, Cole. It's not the first time someone has stumbled across a body out here." Gia lay a hand on his arm and opened her mouth to remind him of the time she'd come across a body beside the river.

"Yeah, well, this body's no stranger, and I'm going to have a hard time convincing anyone that someone else killed him, and I coincidentally stumbled across him out here in the wilderness. If I'm being honest, I briefly considered walking away, but my conscience wouldn't allow it."

"What do you mean?" Walking away from someone who needed help was completely out of character for him. Of course, he'd been acting odd since the day before when . . . Her gaze shot to his. "You know him?"

"Yeah, I know him. And so do you." He blew out a breath. "It's Rusty Bragge."

CHAPTER FOUR

"What are you talking about, Cole?" Gia just stared at Cole. "How can you be sure it's him? You can't even see his face."

He lowered his head, massaged the bridge of his nose between his thumb and forefinger, and let out a long sigh.

Cybil moved close and lay a hand on his shoulder.

When he finally looked up and met Gia's gaze, he patted Cybil's hand, then stepped toward the body. "It's him, Gia. It's Rusty."

Oh, no. No way could this be the same guy who'd fought with everyone in the café the day before. Although, if he acted like that everywhere he went, and if the things Cole had said about him were all true, it shouldn't come as a surprise that he'd pushed someone over the edge. "Who would do something like this?"

He shrugged. "The fact that he's dead doesn't change the fact that he's . . . well, he was . . . a ruthless, spineless, disgusting —"

When Cybil cleared her throat, he stopped mid-sentence.

His already flushed cheeks reddened. "Well, you get the idea."

She'd already gotten the idea when Rusty had spouted off in the middle of her café in front of who knew how many witnesses — witnesses who'd definitely remember the incident once news hit that Bragge had been killed and dumped in the swamp. "Could you have made a mistake?"

"No," he said and sighed. "It's him."

"You're sure?"

"Positive. I'm sorry, Gia." Cole started to pace back and forth, stopped long enough to kick a half-rotted stump, then hopped a few times in pain before resuming his trek.

"Pacing isn't helping anything, Cole. Plus, you're probably messing up the crime scene. Come sit for a minute." She gripped his elbow and guided him toward a fallen tree where Trevor sat with his arm around Cybil, scanned for snakes and other creepy-crawlies, then gestured for him to sit. "You told us what Rusty was like yesterday, but you never said how you knew him."

"No, I didn't."

Cybil elbowed him in the ribs.

"Sorry. I didn't mean to get testy."

"It's all right, Cole, and perfectly under-standable, but I can't help you if I don't know what's going on. You know anything you say is between us." Everyone in the café knew Gia didn't engage in the gossip that ran rampant through Boggy Creek. She might listen, but she never spread rumors.

"I know. It's not that." He lifted his gaze to look past her to the spot where Rusty lie. "Rusty and I grew up together. He lived three doors down from me, and we were inseparable. We played on the same little league team, hung out with the same group of friends, had sleepovers on a regular basis. He was my best friend. At least, I thought he was."

When he stopped talking, Gia squatted in front of him and caught the pain in his eyes. "What happened to change that?"

"I guess I never realized Rusty viewed us as competitors. I was always happy for him, whatever he achieved, even if it was a goal I'd also set for myself. And I thought he felt the same. When I made varsity baseball in ninth grade, he slapped me on the back and congratulated me. When I became captain of the football team, he hooted and cheered louder than anyone. But then . . ." He sucked in a deep breath, shook his head.

"Then the principal found weed in my locker, and I was put off both teams."

Cybil reached for his hand, entangled her fingers with his. "We all make mistakes, Cole."

He jerked his head up to look her in the eye. "But that's just it. I didn't make a mistake. It wasn't mine. Rusty was one of only three people who had the combination to my locker, including me. So, I figured it had to be the other kid, Jim Kirkman, who'd set me up. I turned my back completely on that poor guy over that. Something I'm not proud of."

"It was Rusty?" Gia asked softly.

"Yeah. But I didn't put it together, even after other incidents throughout the years, until I walked into the prom alone. The girl I'd invited, the girl Rusty knew I had a crush on and was going to ask, said she already had a date. And when I walked in and saw the two of them dancing, and Rusty shot me a victorious smirk, I knew it had been him all along."

"Was that the woman who came into the café yesterday? Amanda?"

"No. She came later." He shifted his gaze to Cybil and winced and had Gia wondering if their relationship had moved past the point of friendship.

Now was probably not the best time to ask. She did lift a brow at Trevor, but he simply shrugged. Apparently, he didn't know any more than she did.

The sound of an engine approaching cut off anything else he might have shared. A park ranger pulled as close to them as he could then climbed out of his SUV, surveying the area as he approached. The stocky officer, his dark hair closely buzzed, was unfamiliar to her.

Gia's heart sank. She'd been hoping Hunt or Leo would get there first. She didn't know the officer, and he didn't know Cole, so he couldn't know right from step one that he was innocent. She tried to shake off her apprehension. No one had any reason to think Cole would have killed Rusty.

"I'm Officer Wade Erickson." The officer shook each of their hands, then stuck his hands into his pockets and jiggled his keys. "I understand you folks had some trouble?"

Cole started to stand, but Gia stepped forward. "We found a . . . someone . . . over there."

The officer pinned her with a hard stare, his eyes such a dark brown they were almost black. Then he sauntered at her side to where Rusty lay tangled, took one hand out of his pocket, and held it out to stop her from moving any closer. If his calm demeanor was any indication, this wasn't the first body Officer Erickson had come across. "Wait here."

The ranger walked around the scene, careful to keep a distance from the body. He squatted down, ran a hand through the high brush, and looked toward the body, then stood and stuffed his hands back into his pockets. When he finally did approach Rusty, he donned a pair of rubber gloves. At least it seemed he knew what he was doing and wasn't likely to contaminate the crime scene, though she had a feeling Hunt wouldn't be too happy he hadn't waited for him before examining anything and possibly leaving footprints. But what did she know?

When she turned her head, Cole was beside her, but instead of watching the officer, his gaze had drifted past both him and Rusty to the other side of the river. He frowned. "What in the world . . ."

Harley squatted beside the river's edge, scrubbing his hands together in the water, while Donna Mae stooped over him, speaking rapidly in his ear. If he was listening, Harley didn't seem to respond to whatever she was so urgently trying to convey. The thought he could have killed Rusty flittered through Gia's mind, then flickered right on out again. Even if he didn't approve of the way Rusty had spoken to her, Harley couldn't harm anyone. He didn't have a cruel bone in his body. Whatever he was trying to scrub away, it wasn't blood on his hands. She was as certain of his innocence as she was of Cole's. "What do you think's going on?"

"No idea." But his gaze lingered as Harley scooped water up and over his arms. "I hope he's all right."

"Me too." And once Hunt or Leo got there, she'd yell to him and make sure he was okay. But no way would she call out while Officer Erickson was the only police presence. He might not understand Harley's quirks. And if he tried to bring him in for questioning . . .

Gia shivered, goose bumps dotting her skin despite the intensity of the sun.

"Ma'am?" Officer Erickson stood in front of her, a plastic evidence bag clutched in one massive fist. "Did you find the body?"

"I . . . uh —"

"No," Cole interrupted. "I did. I was walking with my . . . companion when we found Rusty lying there."

His eyebrows winged up. "Rusty?"

"Rusty Bragge."

"You knew him?"

Cole sighed. "Yes. I've known him since we were kids."

"What's your name, please?" Still clinging to the evidence bag, he pulled a notepad and pen out of his pocket.

"Cole Barrister."

"And what is your relationship to the deceased, Mr. Barrister?"

"Like I said, we've known each other since we were kids." Cole raked a hand through his hair and squinted toward his former friend, his gaze a million miles — and probably fifty years — away from the present. "We grew up together in the same neighborhood."

Erickson lifted his gaze to Cole, pen poised above the empty page. "So you were friends?"

Cole squirmed, stuck a finger in his collar, and tugged. "I wouldn't say we were friends."

Where was Hunt or Leo? Gia checked her phone for messages. Nothing. What was taking them so long?

"Then what *would* you say, sir?" The officer kept his gaze leveled on Cole, his expression far from friendly.

Cole's attention snapped back from whatever memories haunted him. He folded his arms across his chest, defiant and stubborn, far from the man Gia thought she knew. "Actually, I've said all I'm going to without a lawyer present."

"So, I guess you don't want to explain this?" Officer Erickson held up the bag for Cole to see. Inside was a receipt.

Gia squinted against the sun's reflection off the bag for a better look. There was no mistaking the All-Day Breakfast Café logo on the top of the receipt. But where had it come from? She'd comped Rusty's meal to get rid of him after he'd put up such a fuss, not that he'd made any attempt to pay his bill.

Cole firmed his lips and said nothing.

Erickson turned the bag around so they could see the back of the receipt — where Cole's name and cell phone number had been scribbled, along with today's date and *8 a.m.*

Sweat beaded along Cole's forehead, dripped down the side of his face.

"Were you supposed to meet with Mr. . . ." Erickson frowned, "Bragge, was it?"

Despite the panic in his eyes, Cole's lips remained firmly closed.

"Could I see that, please?" Gia held out a hand.

Officer Erickson studied her for a moment before taking her name and holding out the evidence bag. But when she reached for it, he pulled it back. "Sorry, you can look, but that's it."

Biting back anything she might regret saying, Gia leaned closer to read the receipt. Apparently, Mr. Bragge had purchased a dozen blueberry muffins at three o'clock on Sunday afternoon. Unfortunately, Gia couldn't tell from the receipt who'd waited on him. She knew it hadn't been her, since she'd have remembered him from that morning. So would any of her employees, all of whom had witnessed the altercation. Unless one of them had served him and shooed him out to avoid another outburst.

So, who'd been working then? Cole had already left. Savannah, Willow, and Skyla would all have still been there, only because they'd gotten so busy. And if she remembered correctly, Earl Dennison — the elderly man who'd been the All-Day Breakfast Café's very first customer and had since become a good friend — had even shown up and lent a hand behind the counter so Savannah could help out in the kitchen. He was the only one who hadn't been present when Rusty had come in that morning. Could he have filled the order? Even if he had, surely someone else would have noticed Rusty. And who'd rung him up? And, most importantly, how did Cole's name and number find their way onto the back of the receipt?

All questions that would have to wait until she could get in touch with everyone. For the moment, though, there was no sense in bringing up anything before Hunt or Leo arrived. "Thanks."

Erickson eyed her, pursed his lips, then tucked the evidence bag into his pocket and removed the handcuffs from his belt. He pointed at Cole. "Turn around and place your hands behind your back, please."

Cole's eyebrows winged up. "What?"

Trevor and Cybil both lurched to their feet. "Hey . . . just wait a minute . . ."

"What are you doing?" A man's voice from behind her made Gia jump.

She whirled to find Harley standing behind her, hand in hand with Donna Mae. In all the confusion, she hadn't seen them come up behind her. How had they crossed the river?

Harley's face reddened. "Why are you arresting Cole?"

Erickson scanned the small crowd — Cole, Gia, Trevor, Cybil, and now Donna Mae and Harley. Apparently realizing everyone assembled was supporting Cole, his hand drifted toward the weapon on his hip.

"Mr. Barrister has refused to answer questions without an attorney present, which is his right. But I will have answers, and if I can't get them here, we'll get them at the station."

Harley propped his hands on his hips. "But he didn't kill anyone."

"Who are you, and how do you know that, sir?" Erickson inched backward, moving himself from the center of their circle to the periphery.

What was he afraid they were going to do? Attack him? Gia's gaze fell on what remained visible of Rusty Bragge. Oh, right. If the officer thought Cole was guilty of murder, and what might be a ring of accomplices surrounded him, she could see where he might be feeling a little uncomfortable.

Thankfully, the short burst of a siren as Hunt pulled his SUV into the clearing interrupted before things could get out of hand — as if they hadn't already.

When Erickson looked toward the arriving officers, Gia grabbed Harley's free hand to get his attention, then shook her head once. Everyone needed to stay quiet until Hunt was the one asking questions. It already looked as if Cole was on his way to a cell — no need to have Harley as a roommate.

Hunt climbed out of the SUV and strolled toward them with Leo beside him. The laid-back stride might fool the casual observer, but Gia knew better. By the time he reached them, he'd have fully assessed the situation and mapped the scene in his mind. With a nod to each of them, he approached the ranger and held out his hand. "Officer Erickson."

"Captain Quinn. It's good to see you, though I'm sorry it's under such disturbing circumstances." Erickson shook the proffered hand, then gestured behind him toward Rusty. "It seems your DOB also happens to be my missing hiker."

"I saw that report this morning." He frowned. "Wife reported him missing, right?"

"Yeah, tried to, anyway. She said he left early this morning to go for a hike and meet up with an old friend, said there'd been some animosity between him and the friend . . ." His gaze shifted to Cole. "So when he was late, she got worried."

"Unfortunately, it hadn't been twenty-four hours, the man wasn't underage, a senior, or mentally impaired in any way, so there wasn't much we could do yet," Hunt admitted.

Erickson nodded. "Still, people can get themselves in trouble out here, so I figured I'd take a look around, make sure he didn't run across a gator or a bear. I didn't expect this."

"No, me neither." Hunt glanced at Cole.

Then, apparently satisfied Leo would mind his suspects and thwart any escape attempts, Officer Erickson pitched his voice low and walked away with Hunt. "Best I can tell, the body was discovered at approximately eight thirty this morning, though the medical examiner will have to . . ."

Gia pounced on Leo. "What is it with that guy? We tried to tell him Cole had nothing to do with Rusty's murder, but he's not listening."

Leo rubbed his chin, grim apology etched on his features. "We'll straighten it out, but you can't blame him. He walked onto a murder scene without knowing any of the players."

She grudgingly acknowledged he might have a point. "But you guys know Cole wouldn't have done this, right?"

"Of course, Gia." He rubbed a hand up and down her arm. "You know we're not going to arrest Cole for murdering anyone."

"Okay, good." Some of the tension seeped

from her muscles. "I'm glad at least you guys know him enough to know he wouldn't hurt a fly."

"Right. That, and Savannah would have our heads if we did."

When her gaze shot to his, he grinned. Well . . . things couldn't be as bad as they seemed if he could find any humor in the situation — not that he was wrong about Savannah. She would definitely make their lives difficult, to say the least, if they arrested Cole.

Her newly found sense of optimism tanked when she spotted Hunt walking back toward them, his expression somber.

When he reached Cole, he stopped. "Hey, Cole. Wanna tell me what happened?"

He rolled his shoulders. "I'd rather not."

Why was he being so obstinate?

Hunt waited a beat. "I'm afraid I'm going to have to insist."

Cole held his hands out in front of him.

Everything went quiet — as if even the swamp's inhabitants sensed the tension and hung on the next few moments. Gia held her breath as Cole and Hunt stared each other down, Leo glanced between them, and Officer Erickson looked on with a satisfied smirk.

With a sigh, Hunt yanked the cuffs from

his belt. The clicks as he closed them around Cole's wrists echoed as loudly as gunshots in the silence.

CHAPTER FIVE

Since the café was closed on Mondays, Gia parked right out front and hurried up the walkway, key in hand. The coming storm painted the air with a greenish hue, and thunder crashed strong enough to rattle the windows. So much for a dry spring. A bolt of lightning sizzled from the clouds toward the park, and Gia hoped Harley had taken cover somewhere safe yet tolerable for him.

She shoved the key into the lock, but before she could turn it, the sky opened up and dumped its contents, soaking her to the bone. Great. She pushed through the door as another rumble of thunder echoed. Even with the air conditioner set higher than usual because they were closed, a shiver crept up her spine and goose bumps rippled across her skin. Not that they didn't need the rain, they did after the dry spell that had apparently just ended, but the storm only added to her sour mood. She left the

Closed sign in the door but didn't bother to lock up. The others she'd invited would be there soon enough.

After turning the air conditioner off, she dropped her purse behind the counter and started a pot of coffee. It didn't appear the storm had any intention of letting up. She thought briefly of running upstairs to the currently unoccupied apartment above the café, where she sometimes crashed and kept a minimal supply of clothing and toiletries, but why bother? The entrance to the stairway was next to the shop, so she'd have to walk outside again to return to the shop anyway.

Savannah whipped the front door open and a barrage of windblown rain ushered her inside. "Yikes! It's a real gully washer out there."

"No kidding."

She brushed water off her clothes onto the mat, wiped her feet, then rounded the counter and hugged Gia tightly. "You okay?"

For just a moment, Gia sank into her embrace, reveling in the feeling of safety only the closest of friends could bring, then she stepped back to reality and gestured for Savannah to sit at the large round table in the back corner. "I'll bring coffee in a minute."

Savannah regarded her for a moment before accepting she wasn't yet ready to share whatever was on her mind and crossing the shop to sit at the back of the table with a clear view of the front door.

Gia took a moment to compose herself while she piled muffins onto a plate. Her first order of business was to figure out who'd waited on Rusty Sunday afternoon. After that, she had no clue what she needed to know. Ultimately, she needed to clear Cole, and the only way to do that was to find Rusty's killer. And Cole didn't seem to be interested in helping himself in any way. She inhaled deeply, the scent of banana muffins and freshly brewed coffee helping to soothe her raw nerves. Okay, the second thing she needed to know was if Cole had been acting strangely lately.

She hadn't noticed anything off before Sunday morning when Rusty had come into the shop. Actually, if she were being honest with herself, Amanda seemed to be the one who'd garnered most of his attention, so maybe she was the one Gia should focus on. She made a mental note to see if she could track down Amanda Bragge and get her to open up about the situation. She ignored the brief stab of conscience that screamed at her that seeking answers from

Amanda would be going behind Cole's back. They needed information to exonerate him, and if he refused to provide it, she'd simply seek answers elsewhere.

Willow and Skyla were next to arrive, rushing inside and waving to Gia as they crossed to where Savannah sat.

Willow paused. "Can I give you a hand with that?"

Gia set the plate of muffins in the center of the table. "I've got it, thanks."

"Sure thing." She narrowed her gaze at Gia, then sat next to her mother.

As the three spoke softly, Gia gathered mugs, plates, and napkins and set them on the table. Once she had everything arranged to her liking, she set two coffeepots in the center of the table and finally sat.

Trevor held the door open for Earl to precede him inside, then followed close on his heels as small hail pinged and bounced off the windows. The scent of the storm clung to them as they took seats.

Though Gia had invited Cybil to join them, she'd declined, saying she wanted to remain at the station so she'd be there if Cole needed her or to give him a ride if they released him. Despite assurances from both Hunt and Leo that they'd drive him home, she'd still refused to leave. "Thank you guys for coming out. I didn't realize when I called that we were going to get such bad storms."

Earl, who sat to her left, yanked off the fisherman's cap he always wore and lay a hand over hers. "Of course we came."

And that simple statement was nearly her undoing. They'd always come. Gia's mother had passed away when Gia was young, her father had provided food and shelter but thrown her out the day she'd graduated high school, and her ex had turned out to be a nightmare. She'd never known what it meant to be part of a family until she moved to Boggy Creek at Savannah's insistence.

No matter how much Savannah had talked about home during the five years she and Gia had lived together in New York, about what it was like to be a part of that community, Gia hadn't completely understood until moving there, until the community, especially her small but growing group of friends, had embraced her, surrounded her, and been there for her time and time again when she'd needed help. And now Cole was the one in need, and she'd do anything she could to help him.

"Thank you." Gia turned her hand over and laced her fingers through Earl's. "I can't tell you how much I appreciate that."

"Any time, dear." He patted her hand, then released her and stood to pour coffee for everyone. "So, what's going on?"

She hadn't brought Earl or most of the others up to date after the morning's discovery, had figured if she got them together she could go through it all only once. "Cole was taken in for questioning in a murder investigation."

"What?" Earl whirled toward her, spilling coffee across the table. "What are you talking about?"

Savannah started to get up, but Willow beat her to it, grabbed a dishrag from behind the counter and mopped up the spill. "I don't understand."

"Why would Cole be questioned?"

"Did he witness a murder?"

"Who was killed?"

The questions pummeled Gia, echoing her own confusion.

Earl set the coffeepot down and dropped into his chair. "Sorry, sorry. I just —"

"Don't worry about it. It's not your fault." She hadn't told them why she needed them to come in, just that she needed to speak to them all and it was important. Apparently, news of Rusty's murder and Cole's . . . involvement, for lack of a better word, hadn't reached the gossip mill just yet. Or if it had, it hadn't reached the All-Day Break-fast Café crew. "I should have told you when I called, but I didn't have the energy to go through it over and over again and figured it would be easier to discuss it with you all in person."

Earl nodded, his coarse, leathery skin creased with worry. "But they can't possibly think Cole had anything to do with killing anyone, right?"

Gia glanced at Trevor, the only one who was privy to what was going on, but he remained quiet, his expression sullen.

"Cole and Cybil found a body in the for-est this morning. Trevor and I were kayak-ing and came across them before they could call the police. When the park ranger ar-rived, Cole was . . ." How could she describe his unwillingness to answer questions? "He wasn't exactly combative, but he wasn't co-operative either. And then the officer found a receipt from the café on the body."

"So?" Savannah frowned. "What does that have to do with anything? A lot of people eat here."

Gia nodded. "I know, but it was Rusty Bragge they found dead."

Savannah paled. "The guy from yester-day?"

"Yeah."

"Still . . ." Savannah smoothed her long blonde hair behind her ear with a shaky hand. "That doesn't mean Cole had anything to do with it."

"Who's Rusty Bragge?" Earl asked.

Gia ran through the story, from the argument in the café to the time they found his body, including Cole's past relationship with him, and ending with Cole's name and cell phone number, along with what the police assumed was a meeting time, printed on the back of the receipt. She pulled out her cell phone and showed them a picture she'd snapped of the receipt. It wasn't easy to read with the sun reflecting off the bag, but the time of the sale showed clearly enough.

Skyla tapped the picture. "That was me. I remember the sale because most people don't buy a dozen muffins from us, and if they do, they're usually a mix, not all one flavor."

Gia's heart soared. "Do you remember what the person who bought them looked like?"

She chewed her bottom lip for a moment, closed her eyes, pressed her fingers against them. When she opened them a moment later, her chin trembled as she shook her head. "I'm sorry. I wasn't paying as much attention as I should have been because we were pretty swamped. I don't even recall if it was a man or a woman. It was the order that stood out, not the customer."

"Hey . . ." Gia squeezed her hand. "It's okay. I just thought maybe we could figure out who it was."

A tear slid down her cheek. "I don't know if it helps, but I do know for sure it wasn't Rusty. I'd have recognized him and called the police the minute he walked in."

Okay, that was something. Considering the number of customers she served on any given day, it wasn't surprising she wouldn't remember one, especially if they hadn't done anything to make them stand out. She'd simply have served one customer and moved on to the next. "Do you remember if the person was alone?"

"I'm sorry. All I remember is thinking it was unusual to order a dozen blueberry muffins. I don't think I noticed anything about the customer who purchased them."

She was already upset enough, so Gia didn't push it. "You don't remember anyone asking about Cole, though? And you didn't write his number down for anyone?"

She shook her head. "No. That's one thing I'm sure of. I never would have given out Cole's number without asking him first."

Gia nodded. Not much, but it was something. She studied the picture of the writing on the back of the receipt. She didn't recognize the handwriting. And since she preferred the old-fashioned way of running her grill, orders were taken by hand on a notepad, so she'd recognize any one of her employees' handwriting. She froze, staring at the words. "This isn't Cole's writing either. So, he wasn't the one to jot it down."

She wasn't sure why that helped, but she couldn't help feeling like it did. Or maybe it was just something to cling to when she couldn't seem to find answers to any of her questions. She'd have to remember to tell Hunt when she next spoke to him. "Does anyone else remember that sale?"

They all shook their heads. Her attention had drifted to Earl, since he'd also been behind the counter working the register, but his expression was apologetic.

"Hey, wait." Trevor yanked his phone from his pocket and scrolled . . . and scrolled. Finally, he held it out to Earl. A picture of Rusty Bragge stared out at them. "I knew I remembered seeing this somewhere."

"Where'd you find that?" Gia studied the image as if it would provide answers. It didn't.

"It was on the community page where I

71

read an article about him opening the deli." He turned to Earl. "Do you recognize him?"

"No. I'm sorry, I don't think I've ever seen him before."

Knowing she wasn't going to get any more information regarding the mystery customer, Gia moved on. "Have any of you noticed Cole acting different lately?"

"You mean before the incident with Rusty yesterday?" Savannah asked.

"Yeah." Since she already knew he was off afterward.

She was met with more head shaking and negative replies.

Savannah took a blueberry muffin, broke it in half, then set both halves on her plate. "So, now what?"

Choosing a random muffin that turned out to be banana chocolate chip, Gia broke it in half and took a bite, not out of any great hunger, though she hadn't eaten all day, but because stress eating was a habit she'd never been able to break. She glanced out the window, where the storm still raged. "Want to take a ride?"

She shrugged. "Sure. Where are we going?"

"Since I can't get any answers from Cole, I figured I'd try to track down Amanda Bragge, the woman who came in with Rusty yesterday morning." Because someone had killed Rusty and dumped him in the forest, and one way or another, she was determined to prove it hadn't been Cole.

Chapter Six

Gia tried to call Hunt before locking up and running to the car. No answer. Nor did Leo pick up when Savannah tried his cell. At least the hail had stopped, but there was no sign the afternoon thunderstorms planned to let up any time soon.

She turned the windshield wipers on high, hit her turn signal, and pulled away from the curb. Thanks to the phone calls Savannah had made to every inn and hotel in the area while Gia had cleaned up, they knew where Amanda was staying. Now if they could just get there before she packed up and went home — wherever home was. "Which way?"

"Make a left at the corner."

Gia did as instructed. Lost in thoughts of murder, she remained quiet as she drove, the steady pounding of the rain and the squeak of the wipers the only sounds. A dull headache throbbed behind her eyes. She really hoped Amanda could shed some light on the situation, because she couldn't come up with a single suspect to offer up in place of Cole. She regretted the thought even as it flitted through her head. Of course, she'd only want to serve up the real killer on a silver platter.

Not that she and Savannah didn't often sit together quietly, but right now the silence was beginning to grate on her. "You're awfully quiet."

"Sorry." Savannah grinned, but it didn't hold its usual humor. "Guess I'm still in shock. You don't really think they believe Cole killed anyone, do you?"

"Hunt and Leo, no. Officer Erickson . . ." She didn't know what to make of the officer's seemingly automatic assumption of Cole's guilt. Okay, that wasn't fair. He'd never accused Cole of murder, just said he had questions. Questions Cole hadn't wanted to answer. "I don't know. Cole wasn't exactly the picture of cooperation."

"Even that seems so out of character for him." Savannah tapped her long, glitter-tipped salmon nails against the door handle, the familiar *rat-a-tat-tat* comforting in some odd way, yet still irritating. She pointed to the road ahead. "There, make a right."

Gia followed her directions, turning onto

75

a narrow palm tree–lined street. The tourists who'd usually flock to the small artsy town must have sought shelter indoors, since the road and sidewalk were barren. Rivers of rainwater coursed down the street.

"The hotel is at the end of the block. You can't miss it."

As Gia inched through the rain, the hotel came into sight. Savannah was right — you couldn't miss it. The enormous stucco building topped by a terra-cotta roof took up the entire far end of the block. Valets and bellhops hunched beneath the arched entryway with umbrellas, ready to greet guests despite the atrocious weather. She let out a low whistle. "This place must cost a fortune."

"No kidding. And if Cole was right, the money belongs to her, not Rusty." Savannah leaned forward, squinting through the waves of water the wipers shoved off the windshield. "And they've been staying here for almost a month when they live right here in the state, though down south farther on the east coast."

Gia's gaze shifted to Savannah. "How'd you find that out?"

She shrugged. "I dated the guy at the front desk for like a minute in high school, and he offered the information."

76

"Offered?"

"Okay, fine, I called and asked." She winked at Gia. "Very sweetly, and he was happy to oblige."

"Uh-huh." Gia tried to do the math as she pulled beneath the overhang, but all it did was increase her headache. "Between staying here and eating out, setting up shop in Boggy Creek must be setting her back quite a bit."

"Huh. Maybe she offed her husband to keep him from squandering her fortune," Savannah said.

As far as motives went, it didn't play for Gia. "Murder seems a bit extreme when she could always have just said no."

"True." *Tap, tap, tap.* It was a wonder Savannah's nails didn't ever chip beneath the constant tapping. "Maybe she killed him for the inheritance?"

"If she could afford a monthlong stay at this place, I doubt she needs whatever little bit of inheritance Rusty may have left behind."

"Still, some people are just greedy," Savannah argued.

"Maybe." While she appreciated Savannah trying to clear Cole, Amanda as Rusty's killer wasn't playing. Not when she'd stood beside him while he'd gone on his rant in the café without so much as a discreet nudge for him to be quiet. "She seemed okay with his actions in the café yesterday morning, but I guess you never know how people act in private. For all we know she could have had it out with him when they left but didn't want to make any more of a scene at the time."

"Could be." But she didn't sound too optimistic.

Gia parked and handed the key to a young woman who took it from her with a smile, then glanced out at the downpour she'd have to run back through after she parked and winced.

Gia kept her voice low. "If it helps, I won't be long. It's fine if you want to leave it where it is."

The girl, Loraleigh according to her name tag, looked around then pocketed the key. "Thanks. I'll keep it here as long as I can."

"Thank you." Gia started toward the entryway, then paused and turned back to Loraleigh. "You don't happen to know Mr. and Mrs. Bragge, do you?"

"Sure." The suspicious looks she kept casting toward the building had Gia wondering if there were cameras mounted somewhere close by. Huh. Maybe she could find out if Amanda had left that morning, if

Savannah's ex-boyfriend had access and was feeling generous. "I heard Mr. Bragge was killed sometime last night or this morning. They found him out in the forest."

News might not have hit the café yet, but it had sure spread quickly enough at the hotel. Hmm . . . she might have to rethink closing on Mondays. "Do you know if they found whoever killed him?"

"Nah, just that they brought some guy in for questioning."

Of course. That would have been too easy. Oh, well. At least Cole's name didn't seem to be spreading yet. "It must have been a shock to hear someone who's been staying here for the past month had been murdered."

"Not really." Twin patches of red flamed on her cheeks, and she looked around again then lowered her voice. "I mean, any murder is shocking, but he wasn't a very nice guy, if you know what I mean."

"I didn't know him." No lie, but Gia wasn't about to spread news of his antics in the café. It was bad enough the Bailey twins had witnessed the altercation.

"Well, let me tell you . . ." Loraleigh leaned closer. "Not to speak ill of the dead or anything, but that guy was rotten. He was mean to the housekeepers, nasty to the valets, had a full-on argument with the manager and tried to get him to comp his stay. He wanted a full month free, just because his room service was cold when he got it. Supposedly. And just between us, I doubt it was even true."

If Chatty Cathy kept talking, Gia might not even have to go see Amanda.

"We all couldn't wait to see him go, to be honest." Her eyes went wide as she realized the implication of what she'd said. "Not that anyone wanted to see him dead, just we wanted him to leave. You know what I mean? Like, go home."

"Of course, I understand," Gia reassured her.

Savannah smiled at Loraleigh, then gripped Gia's elbow, speed-walked her away from the doorway and ducked behind a potted hibiscus.

"What are you doing?"

"Don't look now, but there's a problem at twelve o'clock."

Gia glanced over Savannah's shoulder, then quickly turned away as Hunt and Leo hurried out the front lobby and into the storm. That was all she needed, Hunt finding her out there doing her own investigation. Not that he'd be surprised, but if he saw her and told her to stay out of it, she'd have to go against his wishes to help Cole. It was easier not to be seen. "Now what?"

"Now we avoid running into them. If Hunt sees you here, you're liable to end up on the fast road to divorce before you even make it down the aisle."

That was no lie. She slid deeper into the shadows, she and Savannah huddled together as if in conversation while waiting out the rain. "Well, at least we know Amanda has been notified."

Savannah tracked Hunt and Leo's movement to Hunt's Jeep over Gia's shoulder. "And now we're going to barge in there and ask questions just minutes after she found out her husband was killed."

Gia swallowed any sense of guilt. Cole's life was on the line, but they could give her a few minutes to collect herself. Since Loraleigh seemed to have disappeared while they were in hiding, she and Savannah entered the lobby, strolled through the gift shop.

Savannah checked with one of the receptionists, but it seemed her former beau had gone off shift a few minutes before they'd arrived. After perusing the gift shop, studying the restaurant menu, and doing three circuits of the lobby, Gia gave up. "Do you know her room number?"

"It's about time." Savannah pointed to the

elevators. "Three oh two."

"Come on." They waited for a boisterous group to exit the elevator then entered and pushed the button for the third floor.

"Have you given any thought to what you're going to say to her?"

"Not really." She wanted to find out about the situation with Cole and how it related to Rusty's murder, which hopefully it didn't.

As they exited the elevator and started to round the corner, raised voices had Gia pausing. She held out a hand to stop Savannah in case she hadn't heard. They peeked around the corner. Room 301 stood on the far side of the hall, with the door closed. Directly across from it, a man stood in the doorway of what Gia assumed was room 302, one hand pressed against the door to hold it open.

A woman's voice came from inside the room. Amanda? ". . . don't have even an ounce of decency, Caleb Ryan."

The man — Caleb? — laughed, a wicked laugh that held no sign of good humor. "You want to talk about decency? You're arguing for the wrong person then, Mandy. Because that shop was mine, and you know it, before that no-good, two-timing rat husband of yours bribed that woman on the zoning commission."

"That doesn't give you the right to harass me two minutes after I was notified of my husband's death, or to argue with me when I'm in no mood to deal with this." Silence descended in the hall.

Gia held her breath, scared they'd hear her breathing in the sudden silence.

"Come to think of it . . ." she said softly. "It seems like you knew he was dead before the police even notified me. How is that?"

"Oh, no, you don't. Don't you even try to implicate me, missy." He balled a fist, slammed it against the door.

Gia jumped, startled, and her gaze shot to Savannah. Maybe they should interrupt before this got out of hand. Or even better, dial 911. And tell them what? A man punched a door?

"Rumors have been swirling since this morning that he was killed and dumped in the forest like the garbage he was." Caleb swiped a hand down his goatee, then propped it on his hip and smirked. "And for the record, I have an airtight alibi for last night and this morning."

"Good for you. Now, I'm going to have to ask you to leave. And if you don't, I'll call those two officers back up here and have them remove you — alibi or not."

Gia held her breath. It would definitely

take both Hunt and Leo to remove this guy. He had to be six foot five, at least, and built like a linebacker.

"I'm going, but you'd better think about my offer."

Amanda scoffed.

"Like I told Rusty, I'm gonna get that shop, one way or the other." He stepped back from the door as it slammed shut in his face, then punched it hard enough Gia wouldn't be surprised if he'd broken a few knuckles.

Gia and Savannah stumbled back across the third-floor lobby before he could catch them peering around the corner, witnesses to the threat he'd just made, the threat he'd claimed to already have made to Rusty. But had he followed through? Even if he had an ironclad alibi, he could have hired someone to kill Rusty. That reminded her, she needed to find out how he'd been killed.

He stormed past them a moment later as they pretended to exit the elevator, shoving a hand through his already disheveled hair. The top button of his shirt was open beneath his loosened tie. It seemed Caleb Ryan was having a bit of a day.

His gaze flickered toward them, held, then moved away. His eyes, an unusual shade of mustard yellow, gave Gia the creeps. Or maybe it was the firm clench of his square jaw and the intensity of his stare, or his sheer size. Either way, she had no desire to end up on his bad side, so she simply nodded once as she hurried by.

She wiped a sweaty palm on her leggings, then knocked on Amanda's door. A quick look down the hallway assured her Caleb hadn't returned.

Amanda swung the door open. "I already told you —" She paused when she spotted Gia and Savannah. "I'm sorry, I thought you were someone else."

"We're sorry to bother you, Mrs. Bragge." Gia's hands shook. What was she doing here, knocking on the door of a woman who, at best, appeared to be far from a grieving widow and, at worst, a cold-blooded killer? That wasn't fair. She could very well have killed her husband in the heat of passion.

Either way, Hunt was going to have a meltdown that she'd possibly put his cousin in danger — again. But, as Savannah was so fond of reminding everyone, she was a big girl and made her own choices. It didn't do anything to alleviate Gia's guilt. "I was wondering if I could have a few minutes of your time?"

Amanda narrowed her gaze at Gia. "I

85

remember you. You're that woman from the café in town. Well, if you came to see Rusty, sorry, you're a little too late."

"I —"

She stepped back and started to swing the door closed.

Savannah stepped in the way. "Like Gia said, we're sorry to bother you, but we have a few questions about your husband."

"Doesn't everyone," she muttered as she stepped back and gestured them into the room.

CHAPTER SEVEN

Gia ignored the voice of reason whispering in her ear not to enter the room of a suspected killer and crossed the threshold. Between her and Savannah, they could probably take her if they had to.

Two things hit Gia simultaneously — the mess amid the luxury, and the basket of blueberry muffins in the center of the table. "First, let me say how sorry I am for your loss."

Amanda snorted and strode across the room to the bar in a swirl of pink silk. A little early — or late, depending on how you looked at it — in the day to be parading around in a negligee and robe. Then again, some people would probably find it early for the scotch on rocks she filled to the brim before flopping into an armchair and crossing one leg over the other with a sigh. "Go ahead. Ask your questions."

Savannah quirked a brow at Gia, then

used two fingers to lift a black negligee and a pair of fishnet stockings from the back of the only other chair and set them aside on the dresser, then sat across the table from Amanda, leaving Gia to do the talking.

Gia remained on her feet. Not that she expected Amanda to launch herself out of the chair and kill anyone, probably, but because she thought better while pacing. She did a quick count of the muffins; ten of the twelve someone had picked up Sunday afternoon were still left. The basket didn't look familiar. Had Amanda or Rusty placed them there? Or had someone else purchased them and sent them in the basket as a gift? Then how would Rusty have gotten the receipt? It would be tacky to send it with a gift basket. Of course, being tacky was probably the least of the killer's faux pas.

Amanda cleared her throat, jarring Gia from her thoughts. "I don't have all day, you know."

"Oh, uh . . ." She ripped her attention from the muffins to scan the rest of the room. Clothes littered the floor, wet towels lay in a heap against the open bathroom door, and toiletries were scattered and tipped across the counter. A mostly empty wine bottle and one glass stood on a nightstand beside the bed. On the other nightstand, a wineglass lay on its side, its stem shattered, and the hotel phone hung from its cord over the front. Was Amanda simply a slob? Had she or someone torn the room apart in search of something? Had there been some sort of fight? "I'm sorry to bother you —"

"You said that." Amanda waved an impatient hand and took a long swig of the scotch.

"Oh, right . . ." Gia's thoughts were a jumbled mess. She had no idea what to ask, hadn't thought of anything past trying to help Cole out of this mess. "Mrs. Bragge, do you have any idea who might have wanted to kill your husband?"

She eyed Gia. There was no denying Amanda was a beautiful woman, but those green eyes were cold, calculating, like a predator sizing up its prey. "Probably anyone who's ever done business with him."

Not surprising. Also not helpful. "Do you know Cole Barrister?"

Her bored expression slipped, just for an instant, then the shutters slammed closed again. "What about him?"

"He was taken in for questioning. But if you know Cole at all, you have to know he wouldn't have killed anyone."

"No. The man I knew wouldn't have hurt

a fly." She stared into her drink for a moment, then seemed to shake off whatever memories plagued her. "But that was a long time ago. People change."

"How well did you know Cole?"

She slugged back the rest of her drink, stood, and sauntered toward the bar with a feline grace that reminded Gia of a tiger — smooth, stealthy, deadly. Could this woman have had anything to do with Rusty's death?

"Mrs. Bragge?"

"I thought I knew him very well, once upon a time. But, like I said, people change." She dropped an ice cube in the glass, uncapped the scotch bottle, and poured.

Gia waited.

She lifted her glass and once again turned to face Gia. "Is that it?"

"Did you recognize him in the café yesterday?" Because if his devastated expression was any indication, he'd recognized her immediately.

She set the glass down on the bar with a loud thump. "What does this have to do with Rusty's murder? And why are you here intruding on my grief with this trip down memory lane?"

"Because Cole is a good man, and a very dear friend of mine, and he's being questioned because he was the one to find the bo-o-uh . . .” She paused, shamed by the sudden realization she was talking about this woman’s husband. Grieving or not, she was still a new widow. Maybe the lack of visible grief was shock. “I’m sorry. I don’t know if the police mentioned it, but Cole was the one to find Rusty this morning. And he was very upset.”

“That’s too bad.” Leaving her drink on the bar, she returned to her seat. “But there’s nothing I can tell you. Cole and I dated about a million years ago. And then we didn’t.”

“And that’s it? You don’t even have enough feelings left for him to try to help him out of this mess?”

She lowered her gaze to her intertwined fingers. A sudden burst of sunlight streamed through the window, reflecting brilliantly off her long, coffin-shaped, silver glitter nails. “Whatever happened between Cole and me was over a long time ago, when he left me.”

A gasp escaped before Gia could stifle it. Though Cole hadn’t filled her in about the details of whatever relationship he and Amanda had shared, she’d suspected Rusty had somehow stolen her away from him. “Cole broke up with you?”

"Yes. And that's all I'm going to say. I've spent the past twenty-five years married to a man I despised, thanks to Cole Barrister." She stood, smoothed her robe, and walked to the door. "Now, if you'll please leave. I have matters to attend to."

"Wait, one more thing."

"Yes?"

"If you despised your husband so much, why'd you try to file a missing person's report when he'd barely been gone a few hours?"

A cold, harsh laugh blurted out. "I have no idea what you're talking about, but I can assure you, if Rusty had decided to walk out and never return, the last thing I'd have done was file a police report. With my luck, they might have found him."

Gia glanced at Savannah. When she simply shrugged and stood, Gia started toward the door. "I'm sorry to have bothered you."

Amanda tilted her head, stared at Gia. "Instead of repeated apologies, how about you just leave me alone?"

"Of course." Gia reached for the doorknob, then paused. "Can I just ask one more thing?"

"Last question."

"Why were you with Rusty in my café on the morning before he was killed? And why didn't you make any attempt to stop him from making a scene?"

"That's two questions." She whipped the door open. "Neither of which are going to get answered."

"Thanks for your time." Gia hurried out the door and down the hall with an uncharacteristically quiet Savannah at her side, waiting for the door to slam shut behind her. "Well, that was a waste."

"Oh, I wouldn't say that."

Her gaze shot to Savannah. "What do you mean?"

Savannah glanced over her shoulder then pushed the button to summon the elevator, tapped her toe until the door opened, then stepped inside.

Gia followed, waited for the doors to close, and pushed the button for the first floor. "Okay, spill it."

She held up her hands. "Let me start by saying my theories rely heavily on supposition and lighter on facts."

"Fair enough." Especially since Savannah's instincts were usually spot on. She didn't often say something if she wasn't fairly sure she was right.

"First, what was your take on Caleb Ryan?"

"He seemed angry. Um . . ." With no idea

what exactly Savannah was fishing for, Gia tried to think back. He'd been disheveled, nasty, disrespectful, and seemed to have no empathy for Amanda Bragge. Then again, Gia's sympathy level was in the basement with that woman too. "He definitely threatened Amanda. And it seemed he admitted to threatening Rusty sometime before he was killed too."

"And how would you feel if a man that size came at you like that when you were alone in a hotel room?"

Gia had been nervous just crouching in the hallway when she wasn't even a blip on his radar. "Anxious, I suppose."

"And did Amanda seem anxious to you? Or afraid? Or even slightly nervous?"

She thought back to her pouring the drink. That could be a sign of nerves, though her hands had been rock steady. Even though Gia's own had been shaking by the time she'd knocked on the door. "No. Not at all."

"Hold that thought." She held up a finger. "And what about the condition of the room?"

That, she had noticed. "Amanda is either not much for housekeeping, which is possible considering her supposed wealth if she's used to a maid coming along and

94

cleaning up behind her, or she or someone else trashed the room. You know, before I was thinking maybe someone ransacked the place searching for something. But perhaps someone tossed it in a fit of rage."

"Think harder." Savannah urged her on silently, clearly trying to lead her somewhere. And if that was the case, she had her reasons for wanting Gia to figure it out on her own.

She tamped down the glimmer of annoyance. And then certain things stood out. The wine bottle. The glasses, one on each side of the bed. The sexy lingerie, the stockings, the dress clothes strewn throughout the room. Even the cosmetics spilled across the bathroom counter. "It was all women's belongings."

"Keep going." Savannah rolled her hand as the elevator doors opened on the first floor.

Gia stayed quiet while they crossed the lobby, letting the room's contents swirl through her mind. When they stepped outside, sunshine, blue skies, and puffy white clouds greeted them, though threatening storm clouds still raged in the distance. A huge rainbow painted the sky from one side to the other, and she took a moment to admire the beauty.

"Gorgeous, right?" Savannah asked.

"It sure is."

Loraleigh hurried over, glanced around, and handed Gia her keys. Thankfully, they didn't have to wait since she'd left the car right where it was.

"Thank you." Gia handed her a tip.

"Sure thing. Thanks." With a smile, she bounced off to her next guest.

Gia climbed in and waited for Savannah to buckle her seat belt, then glanced in the rearview mirror, once over her shoulder, and hit the gas. She pulled through the circular drive and headed back toward the road.

"So?" Savannah resumed her nail tapping as if she'd never stopped.

"The clothes all over the room reminded me of our room when we lived in New York and you used to head out for auditions and couldn't decide on the perfect outfit."

"Exactly, you try something on, look in the mirror and realize it makes your butt look big or whatever —"

"Like you ever had that problem."

Savannah grinned. "Just sayin'. Then you toss the outfit over your shoulder some-where and move on to the next. That's how that room looked to me."

"Yes, I can see that." And if that was the

case, where had she and Rusty gone? Or had they planned to stay in? Was that the reason for the lingerie? Then how had Rusty ended up in the Ocala National Forest the following morning?

"But where were all of Rusty's belongings?" Savannah pressed.

"Huh?" Seemed Gia had lost track of Savannah's thoughts.

"Rusty's clothes, shoes, toiletries . . ." she continued. "There were no men's items in that room, and I looked. And yet, I distinctly detected the scent of Old Spice."

No wonder she'd been so quiet, her mind had been preoccupied with this. "So you think Rusty had his own room but met up with Amanda in hers?"

"It's possible, even in a good marriage, that one or both partners would enjoy their own space, especially when they'd been staying there for over a month. Even the closest spouses could get on each other's nerves closed up in a room together all that time."

"But?"

"But it's not jibing for me." Savannah shifted, turned more fully toward Gia. "Why doll yourself all up for a man you despised? I can see her having an ulterior motive for staying married to him, whatever that might have been, but why seduce him?"

True. "When you asked your friend about Amanda's room, did you ask about Rusty too?"

"No, I didn't think of it at the time."

"Maybe you could call him back and ask?"

"I will, in a minute. First . . ." She stopped tapping, and the silence echoed. "Go back to Caleb. Tie open, shirt rumpled, hair disheveled . . ."

A lightbulb dinged on. She wasn't usually so slow to follow Savannah's train of thought. "You think he was with Amanda before she was notified?"

She clapped her hands together. "I do. To me, that argument seemed intimate, more like a lover's spat than a disagreement between two strangers."

"Huh . . ." Now that Savannah had pointed it out, she could see what she meant. But still . . . Savannah was right, it was only supposition. "Do you think he could have been in the room when Hunt and Leo were there?"

"Only one way to find out." She pulled out her phone and scrolled, then pushed a name and put the phone against her ear.

"You think that's a good idea?"

She winked. "Hey, Hunt, I have a question for you, but first let's pretend we did

98

the 'You stay out of my investigation,' 'I'm sorry, it won't happen again,' 'It'd better not,' and blah, blah, blah."

Gia could hear his sigh from her side of the car even before Savannah switched the call to speaker.

"Fine. What gives?"

"When you and Leo went to notify Amanda Bragge of her husband's death, was she alone?"

"As far as I know. Why?"

"Did you happen to notice the smell of men's cologne in the room?"

"No, but I did notice none of Rusty's belongings were present, probably because he had his own room."

At least that much had been confirmed.

"Well, when Gia and I stopped by to offer our condolences . . ."

To Hunt's credit, he didn't even scoff at that.

"A man named Caleb Ryan was at her door, arguing and threatening her."

Gia could hear the *clack, clack, clack* as Hunt typed the name on a keyboard.

"Says here he's a real estate developer."

"That makes sense, considering he accused Rusty Bragge of bribing someone on the zoning commission to get the permits he needed to open . . . huh . . ." Savannah paused, frowned. "Actually, he didn't specify it was the deli, I just assumed it was. He only said shop."

"And she also accused him of knowing about Rusty's death before she'd been notified, but he said he had a rock-solid alibi . . . uh . . ." It hit Gia like a ton of bricks, and she glanced at Savannah.

Savannah grinned back at her. That was the part she'd been waiting to see if Gia would come to.

"Amanda was his alibi."

"Give the girl a prize," Savannah blurted.

"Okay, Lucy and Ethel, this is great information, thank you. Unfortunately, I need a pesky little thing called evidence before I can accuse anyone of . . . well, anything . . . let alone murder. So, you two, go find another sandbox to play in while I try to find proof any of your accusations could be accurate."

"Oh, and see if you can find out who filed the police report, since Amanda swears it wasn't her," Savannah blurted before he could hang up.

"Is that it, boss?"

"For the moment, cous." Savannah was smart enough to disconnect before he could say anything else. She turned to Gia, waggled her perfectly sculpted brows up and down. "So . . . are we going to go play somewhere else?"

"Of course. I just haven't figured out where yet."

She shrugged one delicate shoulder, scooped her hair back, and tied it in a ponytail. "Social media's always a good place to start."

"True, people don't realize they post a treasure trove of information about themselves for anyone with a halfway decent shovel to dig up."

"And then there are those especially valuable gems people think they've buried deep enough to keep hidden." Savannah checked her nails, which were perfect, as always. "The ones that take a more talented hunter with a special set of tools."

They looked at each other and grinned, then said together, "Alfie."

CHAPTER EIGHT

Gia pulled into the driveway of her Spanish-style ranch, shifted into Park, and sat. Sometimes she still got chills when she pulled up to the house. The cream-colored stucco and scalloped terra-cotta tile roof were perfect, and it was all hers. A dream come true.

"You ready?" Savannah climbed out and grabbed the groceries from the backseat.

If Alfie was coming over, they'd need snacks. Plus, she was hoping she and Savannah would get to watch a movie and munch on popcorn, just like they used to do, since Hunt and Leo would no doubt be working late to solve Rusty Bragge's homicide. She got out and started toward the front door, then stopped when she spotted her nemesis sitting atop her garbage pail, digging through a container of shrimp. "Are you kidding me?"

"What's wrong?" Savannah glanced in the

direction Gia was staring just as Gia started toward the side of the house, where garbage was once again strewn across the lawn. She rounded the car until she stood beside the driver's door, then stopped short. "Whoa, Gia, hold up."

Gia paused, one eye on the raccoon and one on Savannah. "What? I have to clean up the garbage."

"Yeah, but . . ." She gave the raccoon the side-eye. "Those varmints can carry rabies and whatnot. You should wait until later when he's done."

Gia lifted a brow. "Seriously? He's just sitting there staring at me. It's like he's taunting me, daring me to try to stop him. If I don't make a stand here, I might never get rid of him."

Savannah laughed out loud — a full-on belly laugh.

"Glad you find my misery so entertaining."

"Gia —" She hiccupped and laughed harder.

But Gia tuned her out as she spotted the garden house hanging coiled on the front of the house and inched toward it, her gaze riveted on the critter, whose head tilted to watch her in fascination, shrimp clutched in his grubby little claw. Sweat soaked Gia's back, and her hands shook as she uncoiled the hose and turned it on, then backed away until the hose pulled taut.

Savannah just shook her head, then opened the driver's-side door and set the groceries on the front seat. "Are you sure you want to mess with this little guy?"

"What choice do I have? The raccoon-proof cans are obviously not doing the trick, but if I scare it off, maybe it won't come back?"

"So, that's your plan?"

"Keep your skepticism to yourself."

She laughed again, leaned her butt against the hood of the car, and folded her arms, obviously settling in to be entertained. No doubt Hunt and Leo would be getting an earful later.

If Gia didn't want to be completely humiliated, she'd better make this work. "Okay, buddy, I'm going to give you one chance to get out of my garbage, and then you're getting soaked."

Rocky Raccoon just stared at her through those big black — adorable — eyes. Great. Now what? She couldn't spray him. Not that it would hurt him, probably, but she couldn't take that chance. She turned the nozzle to the strongest stream, aimed, and opened it up. The spray hit the can with

104

enough force to knock it over, spilling several more bags.

The raccoon startled and shot toward her.

Uh-oh. Gia screeched and stumbled backward, but with her death grip on the hose, it tightened and jerked her back.

The raccoon was still hightailing it straight toward her. Why had she assumed it would flee in the opposite direction?

Savannah bolted toward the house, leaving the car door open.

And in it went.

"Oh, no, you don't." It was bad enough he was making a mess out of the garbage, no way was he getting the groceries they'd just bought.

Keeping the hose aimed in front of her and both eyes peeled for the raccoon, Gia crept toward the open car door. She peered in the side window but didn't see the raccoon. She tiptoed sideways, leaning over to see in the back window.

The raccoon was crouched in the corner of the backseat, back arched, looking none too happy.

With her gaze glued to the creature, Gia grabbed the grocery bags off the front seat, dropped the hose, and ran.

Savannah swung the front door open as she reached it, then stumbled in beside her and slammed it shut behind them. They both leaned their backs against the door — as if the raccoon could open it and follow them inside. Gia started to laugh, then remembered its position, sitting atop the garbage pail, shrimp held between its hands, a little too human-like. She turned and locked the dead bolt.

Thor, her hundred-plus-pound Bernese mountain dog, bounded into the foyer, skidded as he tried to stop on the tile, and plowed into Gia's legs, then looked up at her so adoringly she couldn't help but laugh.

She shifted the bags to pet his big, blocky head. "One of these days you're going to realize you have to stop sooner."

He wagged his entire body as he pressed his side against her legs, keeping her from moving until she'd spent a sufficient amount of time greeting him.

"I know, baby, I'm sorry I'm late."

Thor barked once, then turned his attention to Savannah.

Klondike, the tiniest of the three kittens Thor had saved from a coyote attack, sauntered into the foyer. She'd filled out as she'd grown, her black and white fur and black booties now soft and silky, the chunk missing from her ear the only remaining testament to the ordeal she'd suffered. With too much dignity to pounce as Thor was prone to, she simply weaved between Gia's feet until Gia scooped her up and nuzzled her against her neck. "Hello, little one."

Klondike tilted her head back, stretched, and eyed Savannah as if just noticing her presence.

"Sorry, baby, Pepper's not here tonight. Maybe I'll bring her next time." Savannah had adopted one of Klondike's siblings, and Alfie had taken the other. If the two of them hadn't been so insistent, Gia would have claimed all three.

She lowered Klondike to the floor. She was late, and they needed food and water, then she had to take Thor out. Out into the yard. Where Rocky might be lying in wait to ambush Gia for spraying him with the hose.

When Thor trotted toward the kitchen, Savannah turned to Gia.

Gia just looked at her for a moment, then held up the bags in triumph. "At least I saved the snacks. From the raccoon and Thor."

Savannah blinked twice, then grinned. "So . . . now what?"

Gia trudged to the living room curtains, parted them, and peeked out. Since she couldn't see into the car, she had no way to know if the raccoon was still there. Hopefully, it wouldn't decide to build a nest — or whatever kind of shelter raccoons lived in. Being Gia was born and raised in New York City, she knew little, okay nothing, about wildlife. She supposed she could wait for Hunt or Leo to get off, then ask them to clear the car. But she'd never live that down.

Maybe she should have shut the car door and trapped it inside. She could still run out there and slam the door shut, but then what? She had no idea how long it would take to get someone out there to take care of it, and even this late in the day the Florida sun was too hot to trap a poor critter inside a vehicle. She let the curtain drop and headed for the kitchen. "Now we eat."

Savannah followed. "It'll probably leave once it feels safe again."

"You mean when he realizes the crazy woman with the hose is gone?"

She laughed. "Something like that."

Gia set the bags on the counter, then fed Thor and Klondike while Savannah unpacked the groceries. "What time is Alfie coming?"

Savannah glanced at her phone. "He should be here any minute."

"Did you tell him what was going on?"

"Yup." She waggled her eyebrows. "He said he'd be here with bells on."

Gia paused, Thor's leash clutched in her hand. "You don't think he'll really wear bells, do you?"

Savannah shrugged and stuck the butter in the fridge. "With Alfie, you never know."

"Too true." She usually let Thor run free in the fenced section of the yard, but she didn't want to chance him getting hurt if the raccoon was out there. No matter how affectionate Thor had been with Klondike, refusing to leave her side after he'd rescued her, she wanted to be careful. There was no way to tell how he might react if he felt threatened or thought Gia might be in danger. As soon as he finished eating, Gia clipped the leash to his collar and scanned the yard. "Let's make this quick, boy."

She whipped the door open, hurried outside and kept watch while he did his business, then ran back up the deck stairs and into the kitchen. All without coming across any wildlife, thankfully. She double-checked she'd locked the dead bolt, then washed her hands.

Once they finished putting away what they wouldn't need until later, Gia turned the oven to preheat, then lined up trays on the table. She opened boxes and spread frozen appetizers on the trays. Not the healthiest dinner, but they hadn't had time to eat yet, and appetizers would be easy enough to eat while they researched whatever they could find that might help exonerate Cole. Plus, if Hunt and Leo got off early enough, they could always just heat up some more.

By the time a knock sounded on the front door and Thor took off barking, the table was lined with platters filled with appetizers, drinks had been set out, and two laptops sat open on the kitchen table. She started for the door then paused and glanced at the food. Both Klondike and Thor were occasionally known to try to poach. "Can you watch the food while I go let Alfie in?"

"Sure thing." Savannah popped a mini egg roll into her mouth as she pulled out a chair and sat in front of one of the laptops. "I'm going to start a list of what we're looking for."

"Perfect, thanks." Because her thoughts were so jumbled it would take hours just to sort it all out. She checked to be sure it was Alfie, then opened the door. "Hey, Alfie, thanks for coming."

"Any time." He practically vibrated with energy. As always, despite working from home as a freelance information analyst,

Alfie was impeccably dressed in Dockers and a blue short-sleeved button-down shirt, complete with a pocket protector containing a row of pens and at least one stylus. He hauled in a bag full of what Gia thought of as hacker tools. "Working with you and Savannah is always a hoot."

Thor nudged Alfie's hand with his head, while Klondike feigned indifference from a distance.

"Hey, big fella. Seems like you've grown since I last saw you." He stopped on the threshold, set his bag down, then petted Thor. When he straightened, he inhaled deeply. "Mmm. Something smells delicious."

Gia glanced at her car, the driver's door still standing open, and sighed as she swung the house door shut. That was a problem for a different time. "You don't know anything about raccoons, do you?"

"Only that they're terrifying, with those intimidating black burglar masks." He shivered and hefted his bag over his shoulder, then stopped short. "That's not what you're cooking, is it?"

"What?" She ran through the conversation in her head. "Oh, whoa, no. The raccoon is outside in my car."

"Oh. Whew." He glanced over his shoulder

as if he could see through the door. "Outside is a good place for it."

So much for getting him to go out there and chase the rascal out of her car. "That's what I figured."

He followed her to the kitchen and set his bag on one of the empty chairs, then pulled out his laptop and some kind of square box Gia didn't bother to ask about.

She probably wouldn't understand it anyway, as tech-challenged as she was.

Once he had everything he needed set up to his satisfaction, he filled a plate and sat. "So, what are we looking for today?"

Gia piled pot stickers and egg rolls onto her own plate, then filled a small bowl with duck sauce and another with soy sauce. "We need to figure out who killed Rusty Bragge so Cole will be off the hook."

He stared at her, mouth full, and blinked a few times, his expression blank. "Hmm?"

"Oh, right." She sometimes forgot that, despite being on the computer all day long for work, Alfie tended to lose himself and forget about the outside world. And he never kept up with the news. So, while they munched on pizza rolls and chips with spinach artichoke dip, Gia brought him up to date.

Savannah tapped a notepad where she'd

written a list. "I figured Gia and I could scroll through any of Rusty's social media accounts. And his wife, Amanda's, as well as the guy that I think she was sleeping with, Caleb Ryan, while you try to do a deeper, more intense search."

He nodded eagerly, set his plate aside, and smoothed his brown hair back. Then he scooted closer to the table, cracked his knuckles, and wiggled his fingers before he began banging away on the keyboard. Before Gia had even found Rusty's first social media account, Alfie let out a low whistle. "This guy owns a lot of stuff."

"Oh, yeah?" Gia answered, distracted as she tried to find any kind of accounts belonging to him. Seems someone in business would have at least one site, for advertising if nothing else. Gia tried to keep up on Facebook, Instagram, and Twitter, often posting pictures of different dishes, sometimes adding a recipe or two.

Alfie stared at the screen, a scowl marring his features. "At least, he did own a lot. It seems he's filed bankruptcy more times than I can count."

"You found that already?" Gia leaned over to see his screen.

He pointed to the search results. "Three current cases popped up as soon as I typed his name in the search engine."

"Can you access past cases too?"

"Sure, but . . . hmm . . ." Alfie scratched his head.

"What?"

"I think you might be more interested to know he was arrested for attempted murder."

CHAPTER NINE

"What are you talking about? What do you mean attempted murder? When?" Abandoning her futile search for Rusty's seemingly nonexistent social media presence, Gia scooted her chair closer to Alfie's so she could read along with him.

Savannah dragged her chair around the table and set it on Alfie's other side. "Was he seriously charged with attempted murder? Who'd he try to kill?"

"Allegedly." Alfie pointed a finger in the air.

"Who did he allegedly try to kill?" Gia tried to follow the tabs as one after another popped open, but before she could read more than a few lines and figure out what she was looking at, Alfie had moved on.

"Unfortunately, I can't tell you that. Juvenile records. Therefore, sealed," he answered, distracted.

Disappointment surged through Gia.

"Does that mean you can't access them?"

Alfie winced and tilted his hand back and forth. "Define can't."

Past experience had taught her the expression he currently wore meant he could dig up more, but it wouldn't be by strictly legal means. Who knew? What he'd already found might well not be on the up-and-up, considering all record of the arrest should technically be sealed, therefore inaccessible.

"Though I've got mad hacking skills, your fiancé . . ." He pointed at Gia, then at Savannah. "And your cousin and husband . . . huh . . . it still feels weird to think of you as married, but that's neither here nor there. Anyway, I doubt either of them would be pleased if they found out we . . . uh . . . intruded on Rusty's privacy, even if he is dead. Maybe especially so."

He was right. "You know what? Don't waste time trying to dig any deeper on that topic. I'll ask Hunt when I talk to him next."

"Or Cole might even know," Savannah said.

"For now, let's see what else we can figure out." But she made a mental note to follow up on the information. Gia frowned at the Instagram profile she was currently searching. For a moment, she'd been optimistic she'd finally come across something, only to be disappointed a moment later when she realized it wasn't the Rusty Bragge she was looking for.

"So, what do you want me to research next." Alfie interlaced his fingers, stretched his arms above his head, and arched his back. Then he dug into the chips and spinach artichoke dip.

"Hmm . . . give me a minute to think." Defeated, Gia shifted her laptop aside. With nowhere left to check for any social media accounts Rusty might have had, she was forced to give up. She tilted her head from side to side, easing the ache in her neck. Not that she'd been at the computer long enough to give her a stiff neck, but the tension of not hearing from anyone coiled there. She discreetly checked her phone for the umpteen millionth time. Nothing.

Savannah smiled at her, but it did nothing to alleviate the worry in her eyes. "I haven't heard from Leo either."

Okay, maybe not as discreet as she'd thought. "Are you having any luck?"

Savannah shook her head. "I can't find any accounts in Rusty's name."

"Me neither." She'd start searching Amanda next.

Alfie perked up. "Are you trying to find bank accounts?"

"Nah." Maybe Amanda and Rusty shared social media accounts? Some spouses did, though with Amanda's reaction, or lack thereof, at the news of Rusty's death, it didn't seem likely. Still, it was possible she'd just been in shock. With a renewed sense of determination, Gia picked up a mozzarella stick and dipped it in marinara sauce, briefly wishing she still had some of Savannah's homemade sauce in the freezer. "We're looking for social media accounts."

"Oh." He looked so disappointed Gia almost laughed, but then his eyes lit. "Do you want to look for the money trail? That's what they always do in the movies."

Gia considered it. Maintaining boundaries was always difficult when Alfie was so enthusiastic and eager. It was like walking a tightrope — trying to sustain a balance between wanting to know everything and not wanting to do anything that might interfere in Hunt's investigation. She'd never forgive herself if something she did compromised his case against a killer.

"Let's hold off on looking at any actual bank accounts, or any other accounts that are protected by privacy laws and would be illegal to hack." You had to be very specific with Alfie. "But, you could try to dig up anything you can about Rusty and

Amanda's finances that you can find by legal means."

"Fair enough." He bopped in the chair as he got started. She'd never seen anyone better suited to his chosen profession, or anyone who seemed to enjoy it more. His fingers flew over the keyboard, windows popped open on his screen. He didn't even slow when he glanced at her. "Did you try Myspace?"

"Is that even a thing anymore?" She slid the plate aside and grabbed her laptop.

Alfie paused, scowled at the screen, then shrugged. "I don't know if many people still use it, but it's still up. Even if it's an old account, you might get some information."

"Yup. It's still a thing." With a renewed sense of determination, she typed Rusty's name into the Myspace search box.

Alfie jotted something down on a Post-it note and held it out to her. "Here's my username and password so you can get in. You might find more that way."

"Thanks." She took the paper from him and signed in. A picture popped up of a younger Alfie, standing in front of a cabin at the Haunted Town Festival with his arm around his best friend, Barbara Woodhull, who'd been murdered this past fall. Gia's gaze shot to him.

He sat staring at the image, his expression sober.

"I'm sorry, Alfie."

"Hey, no, it's fine. I mean . . ." His cheeks flared red. "I mean, it's not fine, but I'm okay. Really, I am. Besides, something good ended up coming out of the whole mess, right? More than one something, actually, because now I have you and Savannah and Babe. From tragedy comes triumph, right?"

Gia reached over and squeezed his hand. She had a feeling the grief of losing Barbara would probably always haunt him, but at least he was moving forward now. Adopting Babe, the last of the three kittens Thor had rescued, had helped save him.

"Anyway . . ." He turned his hand over, squeezed hers, then released it and returned to typing. "I haven't used it in years, but I still go in and change the password with all my others every so often."

"You do?" Huh. Was that something you were supposed to do?

"Yeah, why?" He frowned at her. "You don't?"

"I . . . uh . . ." Until that moment, she'd forgotten she'd ever created a Myspace account. She couldn't remember every account she'd ever set up then dismissed because it didn't help her advertising goals

120

or she couldn't figure out how it all worked. She and technology weren't exactly on the best of terms. "No. Should I?"

"Either that or delete the accounts. People don't realize when they create something on the internet, it's there forever, just sitting and waiting for someone like me . . . well, not like me because I wouldn't ever steal information from anyone . . . unless of course it was to help people . . . I mean . . . maybe I should just shut up now and yank my foot out of my mouth." His cheeks flamed beet red. He took a deep cleansing breath. "What I'm trying to say is, when you leave stuff out there and don't regularly protect it, someone with the right hacking skills and less of a moral compass than I have could access that information and use it for their own personal gain, and you might not ever even realize it happened."

She couldn't help but laugh. Alfie was adorable, and she had no doubt, despite the fact that he was capable, he'd never use his hacking skills to hurt anyone. Still, first chance she got she was hunting down all of her abandoned social media accounts and deleting them. But for now . . . "Hey, look at this. Rusty has an old Myspace. He wasn't friends with a lot of people, but Amanda is on here."

She squinted at the small thumbnail, then clicked to enlarge it. Rusty stood alone, the New York skyline in the background. Gia braced for the pang of homesickness, surprised but thrilled when it didn't come.

Savannah stood and stretched, then rounded the table and peered over her shoulder at the list of his friends. She pointed to one. "Kirkman. Wasn't Jim Kirkman the name of the guy Cole had that fight with when Rusty framed him for putting drugs in Cole's locker?"

The name came back to her even as Savannah said it. She clicked on the profile picture, a gangly young man with his arm slung around an attractive brunette. "But this isn't Jim's profile. It belongs to a Rhonda Kirkman."

Heads together, they scanned through Rhonda's posts. "No mention of a Jim, and Kirkman is a common enough name —"

"It's his wife," Alfie said. "Jim and Rhonda Kirkman are married, not that I can be sure Rhonda's Jim is the same as Cole's Jim, yet, but it seems like too much of a coincidence considering everything."

"Absolutely," Gia agreed. "But why would Jim's wife be friends, even just social media friends, with someone who hurt her husband so badly?"

"I don't know, but give me a few minutes and I'll find out." Alfie waited, fingers hovering above the keyboard.

As tempting as the offer was, Alfie's talents were better used elsewhere. "No, leave it for now. Savannah and I can play with this. But there's something else you could look for."

"Sure."

"When Caleb was yelling at Amanda, he mentioned something about Rusty bribing that woman on the zoning commission. Could you see if you can figure out who it might be?"

"Sure thing." He hunched over the keyboard, ready to dive in.

No doubt he'd have the information before Gia could even remember how to navigate the Myspace website. Although, old social media profiles might give her a glimpse of the past, she needed to know what the players were up to now. "Savannah, could you see if you can find any current information for Rhonda Kirkman?"

"You betcha."

A loud thump against the side of the house had them all pausing, their gazes bouncing back and forth.

Thor scrambled to his feet from where he lay by Gia's chair and started to bark.

"What do you think that was?" Gia grabbed a flashlight from the pantry.

"Don't you have cameras?" Alfie looked around the room.

"No."

"Seriously?" He poked his head into the laundry room. "Living out here by yourself you don't have cameras hooked up so you can see what's going on outside the house without opening the door?"

"Not yet." But it was now next up on the agenda the minute she could afford them.

"Well, when you're ready, let me know and I'll help you choose something afford-able and install it for you."

"You can do that?"

He lifted a brow.

Of course he could. "Thank you."

"Sure thing."

Another thud had Thor going ballistic — barking, growling, pacing back and forth in front of the back door.

Gia pulled out her phone.

Savannah put a hand over the screen. "Who are you calling?"

"Hunt."

She frowned. "For what?"

Huh. An image played out in her mind, calling Hunt to tell him she'd heard a noise. Laughing at herself, she tossed the phone onto a pad beside her computer. "You're right. I was just spooked because there's a killer running around out there."

"A killer whose radar you are probably not even on. Yet." Her frown deepened, and she yanked a pistol from her handbag. "Unless Amanda is somehow connected, then maybe I'm wrong."

"When did you start carrying a gun?" Not that Gia was too shocked, considering many people in Florida did, she had just never known her friend to do so or to feel the need. Savannah was the most trusting, optimistic, genuinely happy person Gia had ever met.

"After my kidnapping, Leo took me to the range, helped me get my permit." She looked down at the weapon that looked so foreign to Gia in her delicate hand. "It makes me feel safer, more in control."

Gia only nodded, too choked up to say anything. Her heart ached for some of the innocence that had been stolen from Savannah.

"Do you want to put a leash on Thor and take him out with us?"

Gia shook her head. Even if it was the smart thing to do, she couldn't chance letting anyone hurt him. The gun ought to be protection enough. "Alfie, will you stay with

Thor and call the police if anything happens?"

He hesitated but then nodded.

Thankfully. She didn't want to put everyone in danger. If she knew how to use the weapon, she'd leave Savannah behind too. "Come on. We'll go out the front and around."

Gia cracked the front door and peered out. Her car door still stood open, the interior light no doubt draining the battery. Great. She slid out as stealthily as possible, Savannah glued to her side, gun held ready. As they crept past the car, she peeked in. She didn't see the raccoon. Maybe he'd gone back to the garbage and that's what the thump had been.

A huge shadow eased across the driveway, dashing that hope.

Savannah grabbed Gia's arm and urgently whispered, "Get back inside."

"What?"

"Now." Savannah started backing slowly toward the door with Gia in tow. "I don't want to have to shoot it."

"Shoot what?"

Savannah never got the chance to answer as Gia's garbage pail tipped from the side of the house and a very large, apparently

126

starving black bear lurched around the corner.

CHAPTER TEN

Gia sucked in a breath, would have screamed if Savannah hadn't pinched her arm between her nails — hard. Instead, she caged the breath in her lungs and began to move faster. When they reached the door, they dove inside, and Savannah slammed it shut behind them. "Ah, man, that was close."

Gia sucked in greedy gulps of air.

Savannah did something with the gun — having no knowledge of weapons, Gia had no idea what — then tucked it into her waistband. "You okay?"

Gia nodded. "First the raccoon, now a bear. What is going on out there?"

Hooking an arm through Gia's, Savannah led her across the foyer to the kitchen. "It was probably attracted to the garbage the raccoon left all over."

Speaking of the raccoon, she still hadn't closed the car door when she was out there.

And now she had to worry the bear might decide to take up residence before morning. She sighed. While she loved Florida, she might not be cut out for such rural living.

Thankfully, Alfie had a tight grip on Thor's collar, keeping him in the kitchen where he was safe. "What was it?"

"A bear, in the garbage the raccoon spilled."

"Oh." Alfie released Thor, who bolted straight for Gia, and had the nerve to look relieved.

"What do you mean, oh? Why are you two so calm?" Gia's heart pounded so brutally against her ribs it rocked her back and forth, giving her a momentary wave of motion sickness. She had to calm down. She hunkered down and hugged Thor closer, weaving her fingers into his thick fur.

"You live in Florida, on the outskirts of the forest, you have to expect wildlife." Alfie grabbed a can of soda from the fridge and returned to his seat. "Why don't you just call a wildlife trapper and have him come get the raccoon? Problem solved."

Gia wanted to handle the situation herself, but he was right. She hadn't given any thought to what other, more dangerous critters might be attracted by the garbage spilled all over every day. A chill raced through her. What if the bear had shown up on one of the days she'd been out there cleaning up the spill, or when she'd let Thor out? She should have known better.

"Hey . . ." Savannah lay a hand on her arm. "Don't beat yourself up. Just call someone and get it taken care of. And no second-guessing. You love your home, you just need to take precautions. It's no different from New York."

"Seriously." She offered a tentative smile. "The only wildlife I had to deal with in New York were rats, pigeons, and an occasional alley cat behind the deli where I worked."

"Yeah, but you still carried pepper spray in case of muggers."

"Huh, that's true." Speaking of pepper spray, where had she put that can of bear spray Hunt had given her? Probably in the junk drawer. She used to carry it wherever she went but had gotten complacent over time. Well, on the bright side, if she didn't have it glued to her hand whenever she left the house, maybe she was getting more comfortable with her surroundings. But comfortable or not, she wasn't leaving the house without it again.

While everyone returned to researching the matter at hand, Gia looked up the number for a wildlife trapping agency that offered emergency services 24/7. A baby crying in the background told her they answered from home, at least on the after-hours number. It didn't matter to her, as long as someone came to help. "Do you want to take care of the baby first?"

"No worries. My husband has her; she's just not happy about it. Colic. To be honest, I'm grateful for the few minutes' reprieve." She must have closed a door between them, since the crying became muffled. "Now, how can I help you?"

Gia explained the situation.

"Okay, we can send someone tonight, but it will cost extra. It's probably okay to wait until tomorrow morning, though, since it's not inside the house or anything."

Of course, that meant she'd have to wait until the trapper arrived before she could go to work, since she didn't want to go out to her car until she was sure it was Rocky-free. "How much is it if you come in the morning."

"Six hundred."

"Dollars?" She couldn't be serious. That definitely ruled out paying extra for them to come tonight.

Savannah cleared her throat, then nodded when Gia looked at her.

Ugh. "Fine. Okay, thank you. Can you

have someone come in the morning? As early as possible?"

"Yup, Harvey'll be there around seven."

Which meant she'd be late again. Plus, she had no idea if Cole would be in to open, since she hadn't heard from anyone yet. "That'll work. Thank you. Do I need to be here?"

"Nope. I'll give you a call once Harvey's done."

Gia gave her the specifics and paid with a credit card, then got a promise Harvey would close her car door once he trapped the expensive little critter. In the meantime, she had to figure out how to get to work. "Hey, Alfie, when you leave, could you drop me off at the café?"

"You're going to work tonight?"

"No, but Klondike will be okay here for the night, and I can take Thor and stay in the apartment above the café tonight. Then I'll drop him off with Zoe at the doggy day-care in the morning before work." And when she came home, hopefully, she'd be raccoon- and bear-free.

"No problem, I'll drop you off on my way home."

"For now, though, lookie what I found." Savannah waved a Post-it back and forth. "I couldn't come up with any information about Jim Kirkman after about ten years ago, but I think I found Rhonda living in Orlando."

"Really?" Gia looked at the phone number Savannah had scrawled on the Post-it and handed her, then glanced at the clock. "You think it's too late to call?"

Savannah shrugged. "What are you going to call her for?"

"Maybe Jim will be there, and we can get some information about Rusty from him."

"Or you could ask her about why she's friends with Rusty on Myspace," Alfie suggested.

"Good idea." She jotted down the questions she wanted to ask, glanced at the clock again, and cringed. Oh, well, nine o'clock wasn't *that* late. Hunt and Leo weren't even off work yet. Instead of trying to justify it any further, Gia made the call.

A woman answered on the first ring. "Since it's after eight o'clock, this had better not be a telemarketer."

"No, it's not, ma'am. I'm sorry to bother you, but I'm trying to reach Jim Kirkman. Is this Rhonda?"

Silence greeted her while she did a quick scan of the questions she'd listed.

"Hello?" Nothing. Gia glanced at her phone screen. The call had disconnected. It could have dropped. She didn't get the best cell phone service at the house. She walked to the front door, reached to open it, thought better of the idea and stood next to the front window instead, then redialed Rhonda's number.

Once again, she picked up on the first ring. "Don't call here again."

"Wait, please. It's important that I speak with you or Jim."

But Rhonda had already disconnected. So much for that lead. Maybe the detectives would do better.

"Did you get her?" Savannah asked from behind her.

"I got her, but she hung up before I could ask her anything." If the woman lived in Orlando, maybe she could run down there and speak to her in person. It would only take an hour each way driving, plus however long it took to get her questions answered. And if Rhonda blew her off as quickly in person as she had on the phone, it wouldn't take more than a couple of hours altogether.

"Well, we can leave that alone for now." Savannah threw a few potstickers on a plate then stuck them in the microwave. "We don't even know if Jim has anything to do with this. It was a long shot reaching out to him."

"True." Gia picked up an egg roll, held it in her hand while she debated the merits of taking the time to visit Rhonda in her mind.

"But Alfie found something . . ." Savannah snatched an egg roll, popped it into her mouth, then licked her fingers. "If you're done contemplating your options there."

It was great to have a friend who knew you so well — usually. "Yup. I'm done." Though she still didn't know what she was going to do. "What'd he find?"

"I'll let him tell you."

Probably a good idea. Alfie was always so eager to help and found great joy in discovering answers. She didn't want to rob him of the opportunity, no matter how badly she wanted some way to move forward.

When she sat next to Alfie, Thor dropped his big head into her lap and watched her through those loving big brown eyes. "Savannah said you found something."

"Yeah. A wealth of financial information, and I do mean wealth."

"I thought you weren't going to check their accounts?" Though she wouldn't complain if he'd decided to on his own.

"I didn't need to. Rusty Bragge might make repeat appearances in the bankruptcy courts, but his wife is definitely not cut from the same mold." He pointed to a list he'd

135

made in a Word document. "I emailed this to you so you'll have a copy if you need it for anything, but that woman is a real estate mogul. I've compiled a list of everything I could find that she owns, either in her own name or through various companies, and it is extensive."

"So, what? You think she makes like millions?" And how did Rusty keep filing so many bankruptcies if his wife was loaded? Not that she was responsible for his debt, but still . . .

Alfie gawked at the numbers on the screen. "Try billions."

"Bill . . . uh . . ." But that didn't make sense. "How does Rusty get away with filing bankruptcy over and over if his wife is worth all that money?"

Alfie just shrugged. "I'm sure she has a great attorney and a whole office full of accountants. But that's not all I found. Here, look at this."

Gia sipped her Diet Pepsi while he brought up a new window.

"I also had a chance to look at the zoning commission. Caleb said Rusty bribed a woman on there, right?" He looked at her for confirmation.

She nodded, the food beginning to sit heavily in her stomach. Or maybe that was dread.

"Well, there's only one woman on the board." A click of the mouse brought up an image of an attractive middle-aged woman with bleached blonde hair and muddy brown eyes. "Brynleigh Colton. She's been on the commission forever and is also the treasurer."

"Bingo," Savannah whispered.

"So she's taking bribes in return for favors."

"She must be taking a lot of bribes, if her lifestyle is any indication," Alfie said.

"What do you mean?"

"The woman lives on a sprawling thirty-acre estate, complete with stables, swimming pools —"

"Pools? As in more than one?"

"Three according to the listing on Zillow. One of them indoors."

"Wow." That was probably even bigger than Trevor's mansion.

"No kidding." He switched to another tab and popped a pizza roll into his mouth, then pointed to the screen.

Gia scanned it and summarized for Savannah. "According to her LinkedIn profile, she's been on the commission for more than twenty years and is also a real estate developer."

"Seems like a conflict of interest to me," Savannah said.

"Plus, I'm sensing a theme. Rusty, Amanda, Caleb, and now Brynleigh, all connected to real estate somehow." Gia stood and started gathering empty plates. Seemed Hunt and Leo weren't going to make it after all. She texted Hunt to let him know she was going to spend the night at the apartment, and if he showed up in the middle of the night when he got off, as he was sometimes prone to do, she could always run downstairs and make him something to eat.

"And, with the exception of Rusty, all of them are extremely successful." Alfie tapped a few keys. "I didn't get time to do much of a search on Caleb, and he's nowhere near as well-off as Amanda or Brynleigh, but he's no slouch either."

"But how do they all connect?" Gia loaded the dishes into the dishwasher. She needed time to think, to figure out how these new tidbits of random information might lead to Rusty's killer.

Alfie stood, stretched, started to close his laptop, then paused. "Do you want me to dig any deeper?"

Did she? Probably, but not tonight. Since she had no idea if Cole would make it into work in the morning, she'd have to get up early and get into the café to prep everything. "At some point I'll want to know more, but if you don't mind, I'd like to get going. I'm shot, and I still have to go to the apartment, and I want to try Cole and Hunt before I go to bed."

He hooked a thumb toward the garage. "What are you going to do about the garbage outside?"

"I'm not going out there in the dark to clean it up, especially without knowing where the raccoon and the bear are. I'll take care of it tomorrow after the trapper comes."

"Come on." Alfie started packing up his things. "I'll drop you off too, Savannah."

Since Savannah only lived down the road, it wouldn't take long. But Gia couldn't help but notice she didn't say she didn't want to put Alfie out and that she'd walk, as she once would have.

CHAPTER ELEVEN

Gia waved to Alfie, then shut the door behind her and smiled when he tapped the horn in response. He'd come to be a good friend, one of many she'd found since moving to Boggy Creek. She unlocked the door to the one-bedroom apartment above the All-Day Breakfast Café, then hurried up the narrow staircase. Since none of her tenants had worked out, Gia hadn't bothered to look for a renter in a while. She probably should — she could certainly use the extra income — but she liked the convenience of being able to crash there when necessary. Plus, if she were being honest with herself, she didn't trust strangers enough to take the chance. It was a flaw she'd have to work on over time, but for now . . .

She paused outside the door to sort through the keys on her ring, and Thor nudged against her side. "Sorry, boy. I guess I should have had it ready."

When her cell phone played a snippet of "I Need a Hero," an inside joke between her and Hunt since he was always trying to protect her, whether she wanted him to or not, she forgot about the key and grabbed the phone. "Hunt?"

"Yeah, sorry it took so long to get back to you. It's been a bit of a day." If the exhaustion she heard in his voice was any indication, he wasn't exaggerating.

She leaned her back against the wall, heart racing, phone clutched in a white-knuckled grip. "What happened?"

"We questioned Cole for hours —"

"You can't possibly think he killed Rusty Bragge," Gia blurted.

Hunt only sighed.

She cringed. It's not like they hadn't been down this road before — Hunt grilling a suspect, Gia feeling sorry for said suspect and insisting on his innocence. "Sorry."

"No, it's all right. You're not wrong." He paused, and his police radio crackled in the background, though she couldn't make out the words.

"Do you have to go?"

"Huh? Oh, no, it's fine. Like I said, you're not wrong. Until today, I'd have bet every dime I have on Cole's innocence."

"But now?" She held her breath. No way

141

could Cole be a killer. Despite all of the trust issues she still battled, she believed in him. If she found out now that trust had been misplaced, she might well lose all faith in her judgment. She reprimanded herself even as the thought flitted through her head. No way would she believe he was guilty.

"I think he's hiding something," Hunt admitted.

Unfortunately, Gia had the same feeling. She just didn't think it pertained to Rusty's murder. "Are you off for tonight?"

"Yeah, I'm headed home now."

"Have you eaten anything?" Though she had no food in the apartment, it would be easy enough to run down to the café and make him something. Truthfully, she could use something herself. Appetizers for dinner hadn't quite eased her hunger but had left her slightly queasy. Or that could be stress.

"Not for a while."

And suddenly, she wasn't quite ready to hear what had gone on with Cole to raise Hunt's suspicions, needed a few minutes to prepare herself for whatever he might say. "I'll tell you what. I'm at the apartment. Why don't you come by the café, and I'll make us a couple of omelets and we can sit and talk?"

"You're sure you don't mind? I know you

have to be up early."

"Nah, don't worry about it." It wasn't likely she'd be able to sleep anyway when her brain was so ramped up. "Honestly, maybe it'll help me unwind enough to at least get a few hours of shut-eye."

"That'd be great, Gia, thank you. I just have to run down a quick lead, and I'll be there. Say . . . half an hour or so?"

Perfect, just enough time to get Thor settled, since she couldn't have him in the shop. "Sounds good. I'll see you in a few."

Once she hung up, she slid her phone into her leggings pocket and unlocked the door. "Come on, boy."

Thor bounded into the apartment ahead of her, then ran around sniffing everything in sight as if he'd never been there before. Seemed he was strung just as tightly as she was.

She filled a bowl with water and set it on the kitchen floor, then considered making herself a cup of chamomile tea to settle her nerves. Better to wait until later, after Hunt had imparted whatever bad news she suspected was coming and headed home. She bent to mop up the water Thor spilled when he drank. "Boy, why can't you just drink it over the bowl, instead of —"

A loud crash interrupted.

Thor barked. He ran to the front windows that looked out over Main Street. Had there been a car accident? Hunt!

Gia ran for the front window, shifted the blinds aside, and peered out. Nothing she could see. Streetlights illuminated the quiet street. No sign of an accident or anyone in distress. So, what had that sound been? She petted Thor's head.

Though he paused and stopped barking for a moment, the instant she removed her hand from his head, he resumed pacing back and forth in front of the window.

"It's okay, boy." She was headed downstairs anyway, and since the stairway door opened onto the sidewalk, she'd have to go outside to get to the shop. She'd look down the street for any signs of activity that might be out of her line of sight from the apartment window.

Reassuring Thor, then locking the door behind her, she jogged down the steps, then cracked the door and peered out before opening it all the way. Huh. Nothing. The humidity punched her in the chest when she stepped out and turned to lock the door behind her. She still hadn't fully adjusted to the thick heat that would rob you of breath for an instant when emerging from an air-conditioned building. Who knew? Maybe she never would.

With Thor tucked inside, and two locked doors between him and any danger, Gia walked to the curb and looked up and down the street. A couple strolled along the sidewalk a ways down, holding hands, occasionally stopping to peek into the window of a closed shop. Tourists? Maybe they'd arrived late and were scoping out places to visit in the morning. Surely, if anything had happened, they'd be aware and not chatting so leisurely.

She followed the walkway the few steps to the café, then stopped short at the gaping hole in her front door. Not again. She had to be seeing things, a flashback to when she'd first opened and someone had broken into the café by throwing a cinder block through the glass door. This time, she'd get a different door, maybe wood or fiberglass on the bottom and glass only on top so intruders wouldn't be able to crash through and crawl inside. Intruders —

Her blood ran cold. The crash had only sounded a few minutes ago, which meant there was a good chance whoever had broken in was still there. She fumbled the phone out of her pocket, almost dropped it from her slick, sweat-soaked hand, then recovered and dialed nine-one-one. She reconsidered even as it rang. Maybe she should have called Hunt directly. That might be quicker. But he'd been going to follow a lead, so there was a chance he wouldn't answer. And she had no idea where Leo was.

"Nine-one-one. What is your emergency?" The operator interrupted her thoughts. Probably for the best.

"I'm at the All-Day Breakfast Café on Main Street in Boggy Creek, and someone broke in."

"Are they still there?"

"I-I . . . uh . . . possibly. I heard the crash a few minutes ago from the upstairs apartment, then I came down here and found a hole in the door."

"Where are you now, ma'am?"

"Standing on the sidewalk out front."

"Can you get somewhere safer? Back up to the apartment or into your car?"

"If I do that, whoever it is might get away." She stepped to the side of the window, anyway, out of view of anyone who might be inside.

"Are you carrying a weapon?"

"No, I'm not." She'd left her purse with the bear spray upstairs, and her leggings only had a side pocket big enough for her phone. Hands shaking, she slid keys be-

146

tween each of her fingers. The key to the back door made her pause. What if the intruder went out that way while she was cowering out front? She clutched her key chain tightly, keys protruding from between her fingers — the best she could do for a makeshift weapon under the circumstances.

Pressing her back against the front wall of the historic, pale yellow building that housed her shop on the corner of Main Street, she listened intently. Thor's barking, muffled through the walls, drowned out any other potential noise. She struggled to block the sound, difficult knowing how distressed he must be, and listened for any sound the intruder might make, wrestling with the decision of whether to peek inside or wait for the police. With all the racket Thor was making, the intruder had most likely already fled out the back.

The sound of tires against the pavement, too slow to be police officers responding to a potential burglary in progress, drew her attention.

A gray sedan pulled against the curb beside her, and a uniformed man climbed out. "Is everything okay here, ma'am?"

Gia's heart stuttered when she recognized him from the crime scene in the forest. "Officer Erickson, right?"

147

"Wade is fine. And you're Gia Morelli. We met earlier today." He frowned and gestured toward the makeshift weapon gripped in her hand. "Is something wrong?"

"Since when do park rangers respond to burglary calls in town?"

"Burglary?" He yanked a pistol from the holster on his belt but kept it lowered at his side. "I was just driving past on my way home and saw you against the wall looking terrified, so I stopped to see if you needed help."

Okay, terrified was a stretch. Probably. And was she supposed to buy he just happened to be driving by? Quite a coincidence if you asked her. Although, to be fair, he had found a receipt from her café on Rusty's body that morning, so was it really a stretch to think he'd scope out the area on his way home? It was probably the exact same thing Hunt was doing at the moment somewhere else. "I'm sorry. I'm a bit jumpy. I was upstairs in the apartment when I heard a crash and came down to find someone had broken in."

"Do you have the key?" He held out a hand.

A reasonable request, yet Gia wasn't happy about parting with her only source of defense. Her hand shook as she sorted out the key to the front door and handed it to him.

"Wait here." He opened the door and disappeared inside.

Gia inched closer to the glass and peered in the door.

Wade did a slow, thorough assessment of the front room, checked behind the counter, then eased the swinging door open into the back hallway where the kitchen, her office, and a storage closet were located. He strode back into the dining room a moment later and flipped on the overhead lights, then opened the door and held it for her to enter. "Whoever was here is gone now."

She hesitated on the threshold, not sure she should enter and mess up any evidence.

"I assume you already called the police?"

The red and blue strobe effect of the first arriving patrol unit bathed the storefront just as Hunt and Leo pulled up.

Hunt reached her first and eyed Officer Erickson before returning his attention to her. "You okay?"

"I'm fine." She resisted the urge to slip into his arms and lose herself for a little while. It was hard to ignore reality when she was standing at her second crime scene of the day.

Wade Erickson held out a hand, which

Hunt shook. "I decided to cruise past here on my way home, just check things out after finding that receipt today, and I found her outside, back against the wall, clutching her keys as a weapon. It almost looked like she was debating going inside, so I figured I'd better stop."

Hunt massaged the bridge of his nose.

Gia schooled her expression to look innocent, she hoped. She hadn't gone in, and that's all that should matter.

"Whoever it was went out the back, left the door standing open." Wade held the door for Hunt.

"Thanks, man," Hunt finally said, then walked inside. He returned a moment later and ushered Gia through the broken glass scattered across the distressed bamboo flooring. He then directed the crime scene technicians to begin their work. "Why don't you come sit down and tell me what happened, then you can walk through and tell me if anything was stolen."

"Can I at least make you something to eat?" The thought of even smelling food had her stomach rolling over.

He pulled out a chair at a round table in a back corner of the café. "I can wait until we're done here."

"Sure." She sat, surveying the damage to

the front door, which would need to be cleaned up and repaired.

Wade waited for Hunt to turn the chair next to her and straddle it, then gestured toward a free chair. "If it's okay with you, I'd like to hang around, maybe follow the investigation. It's not often I get to investigate a murder, and I'd like the experience."

"Sure thing." Hunt pulled out his notepad and focused on Gia. "Okay, what happened between the time I hung up with you and the time the nine-one-one call came in only a few minutes later?"

Gia ran through the course of events, ending with Wade showing up.

Then he put in, "By the time I entered, whoever had been here was gone. I didn't see any sign of anyone, might have even thought it was just vandalism if not for the back door standing open."

"Hunt?" Leo interrupted.

"What's up?"

"The techs just dusted the back door, and they didn't find any prints on the handle or the door itself."

"You mean no prints that didn't belong there?" Gia's prints had to be there. She'd taken her gloves off before opening the back door to throw the garbage in the dumpster before they'd closed after meeting with

151

everyone in the café.

Leo shook his head. "Nope. I mean no prints at all."

"It was wiped," Hunt said.

"Yeah. And that's not all." Leo gestured toward the back of the shop. "You're going to want to see this."

CHAPTER TWELVE

Hunt stood with his hands on his hips, his expression too neutral for even Gia to read, and stared down at the business card lying in the café's back parking lot. What appeared to be a partial footprint marred one half of the card, and one corner was torn. Rusty Bragge's name, printed in bolded black and gold, practically jumped off the white background.

Leo squatted beside the card and lifted it with tweezers, then slid it into an evidence bag and handed it to Hunt.

Gia opened her mouth to question him, but Hunt gave one discreet head shake, and she snapped it closed again. Not only were techs still lingering in the parking lot, but lookie-loos had already begun to gather around the perimeter. One overeager reporter was even trying to sweet-talk her way past the patrol officer tasked with keeping the growing crowd back.

Gia's mind raced. Just because the card was found right where Cole always parked didn't mean he'd been the one to drop it. She glanced at Hunt, desperately trying to read his mind. He turned the card over, studied it, then handed it back to Leo. She could only hope the fact that they'd already released Cole meant they believed in his innocence and wouldn't pick him back up again to question him about the business card.

To his credit, Wade hung back, careful not to intrude on the scene until Hunt waved him over. "Did you go out into the lot when you found the back door open?"

He shook his head. "I just stepped outside the door. When I didn't see a suspect and had no way to tell what way he might have gone, I returned to the front to stay with Gia until help arrived."

Hunt nodded, his expression furiously unreadable. "All right, Gia, let's walk through and see if anything's missing."

"Mind if I tag along?" Wade asked.

"No problem." Hunt and Wade hung back, chatting quietly between themselves, following her as she started in the dining room.

It seemed the register would have been the most likely target if someone was looking to rob her. She slid behind the counter, looking around as she did so. Empty glass cake dishes dotted the counter that ran up one side of the shop, waiting for her to stock them with muffins come morning. Clean bus pans lined the shelves beneath the counter. Coffeepots and the cold brew machine stood on their own shelves behind the counter, clean and ready for the morning. Nothing seemed out of place.

Even though the register drawer was closed, the tray with the change for morning tucked away in the safe in her office, she opened it and checked anyway. Nothing amiss. After a quick run through the rest of the dining room, she did a thorough search of her office, checking the personnel files she kept in a locked file cabinet after the last time someone had broken in and ransacked her office, compromising personal employee information. The drawers were locked up tight. "I don't understand. Nothing seems to be missing. Or damaged."

"Whoever broke in could have opened the register, seen it was empty, then taken off out the back door." Hunt took a seat at one of the counter stools and gestured for Wade to sit as well.

"Or maybe . . ." Wade paused and waited for Hunt to signal him to continue. "The first thing I noticed when I entered was the dog barking upstairs. And it sounded big. Maybe the perpetrator didn't know the upstairs apartment was occupied, then got spooked by the dog."

Hunt pursed his lips. "Could be."

As soon as she could break free, Gia was headed straight upstairs to hug Thor and bring him a treat. "Can I make coffee?"

"That would be greatly appreciated." Hunt grinned.

Gia filled three filters with coffee, added water, then turned all three machines on. Surely Hunt wasn't the only officer in need of fuel. She debated having a cup of her own. Since the café was closed on Mondays, Tuesday mornings required a heavier than usual prep. At this point, she probably wouldn't get any sleep at all. "Do you know if Cole is planning on working this morning?"

Hunt tapped his pen against the counter, very reminiscent of Savannah's nail tapping, a habit she and Hunt shared while thinking. The way the two of them often bickered, they'd probably be appalled to realize how much alike they were.

The thought brought a smile.

"I wouldn't count on him being in too early."

That knocked the smile off her face. "You can't really think —"

He held up a hand to ward off her argument. "What I think is irrelevant. I still have to question him about the business card."

"But don't you think it's more likely the intruder dropped the business card when he ran out the back door?" The image of the card lying in the lot, partial footprint clearly visible, almost as if . . . Inspiration struck. "Besides, the card was perfectly dry and mostly intact, which it wouldn't have been if Cole had dropped it before he found Rusty's body and was taken in for questioning, considering the drenching rain we had. Even if it wasn't soaked, it'd have water damage."

A smile played at the corner of Hunt's mouth, but he didn't confirm or deny her observations.

"Can I just say something?" Wade offered a tentative smile. "I don't know Cole, but Gia seems to be awfully fond of him, as do you. And I don't know Gia or you, but I have to assume you wouldn't have made captain without being a good judge of character. That said, do you think it's possible Cole is being framed?"

Hope surged through Gia. If Wade could see that so clearly without knowing any of the players, surely Hunt had also come to the same conclusion. But Hunt wasn't the problem. He'd have to convince the DA not to bring charges if evidence continued to pile up, or if something less circumstantial pointed in Cole's direction.

"Anything's possible." Hunt straightened as Gia set an oversized mug in front of him. "Thanks. It's too late and there's too much commotion to make omelets now, but do you happen to have any muffins lying around?"

"Oh, yeah, sure." She set out another mug. "Coffee, Wade?"

"Thanks, I'd love some."

She filled mugs for both him and Hunt, then set the pot back on the burner. The acid burning in her stomach and creeping up her throat would only be worsened by drinking coffee. "Is it okay if I go into the kitchen for the muffins?"

Hunt waved a hand toward the kitchen, still frowning at his pad, or more likely something going on in his head that only he was privy to. "Yeah, go ahead."

She headed for the back. As much as she wanted to question Hunt, wanted to discuss what little she, Savannah, and Alfie had found, wanted to find out if Cole had mentioned Jim Kirkman, wanted to ask if

158

he'd found anything more about Caleb Ryan or the woman he'd bribed on the zoning commission — allegedly — she'd wait until there weren't a million witnesses buzzing around.

So, instead of concentrating on the investigation, Gia plated muffins and served coffee. By the time everyone cleared out, there wasn't much sense in going to bed. It wouldn't be her first sleepless night, and sad to say, probably not her last. After bringing Thor his treat and spending a few minutes reassuring him all was right with the world, Gia returned to the café to start prepping, which would all be up to her since Hunt had left the café to head to Cole's.

Hopefully, this time, the stubborn old coot would cooperate and make things easier on everyone, including himself.

Gia checked her list. She needed both banana chocolate chip and blueberry muffins. May as well start with the banana, since that would probably be all the breakfast she'd have time for. After preheating the oven, she added flour, baking soda and salt to a stainless-steel mixing bowl and set it aside. While waiting for the butter to melt, she mashed overripe bananas. The sweet scent made her stomach growl, increasing the burning sensation. She ignored it. After she got things in order to open, she'd have a muffin and a cup of lemon ginger tea.

Once the butter melted, she whisked in the brown sugar, then added eggs, vanilla, and the mashed banana and tossed in the chocolate chips that were left in the container. Dang — not enough. The thought of leaving them as is flittered through her head, and she shoved it right back out again. She hadn't worked so hard to make a good reputation for her café only to chintz out on the chocolate chips because she was too lazy to go to the storage closet for more, no matter how exhausted she was.

With a sigh, she stripped off her gloves, tossed them in the trash, and crossed the narrow hallway to the storage closet. If Cole did manage to get into work today, she might well go upstairs for a twenty-minute power nap. It was probably the only way she'd make it through the day.

She opened the door and flipped on the light. Not that she couldn't find the chocolate chips, or anything else, in the dark, thanks to her meticulous organization, but there was zero chance she was walking into a dark room in Florida. A shiver raced through her as the image of the furry, black and orange spider scuttling across the bathroom floor, eerily fast, flashed into her mind. Of course, the image of Hunt, along with half the Boggy Creek police department, bursting into the bathroom, guns drawn, at the sound of her scream made the incident slightly less horrific. Or maybe more so. She hadn't yet decided.

She laughed at herself, her severe arachnophobia only allowing her to find humor in the situation because there were currently no spiders of any sort in attendance. She grabbed two bags of chocolate chips — may as well fill the container so she wouldn't have to keep coming back — then started to turn. A flour canister on the bottom back shelf had been turned and hung just a bit off the edge. Someone must have banged into it. But whom? No way would Cole have left it that way; he was just as particular about running an organized kitchen as Gia was, if not more so. Maybe Savannah, or Willow, or Skyla had grabbed something off the shelf and knocked it over.

She twisted the canister and started to push it back into place, when she noticed a large black lump hanging beneath the shelf along the back wall, nearly concealed in shadow. She squealed and danced back. *Please, don't let it be a spider, please, don't let it be a spider.*

Run or find out for sure? If she ran, and

then returned with someone else and it was gone, she'd be freaking out all day waiting for it to come scuttling out of every shadow. No way was she dealing with that.

She backed up to the doorway and set the chocolate chip bags on the shelf closest to the door. If that thing so much as twitched and she ended up having to make a run for it, at least she could grab the chips before slamming the door shut and giving herself, however briefly, some illusion of safety. She took a couple of calming breaths, unscrewed the handle from the broom hanging on the back of the door, then inched forward. Using the long pole, she shifted the canister out of the way and bent to get a better look. When she couldn't identify the dark lump, she moved closer, narrowed her gaze. Whatever it was, it seemed too big to be a spider — she prayed — because if it was, she was filling her car with gas, pointing it north, and heading straight back to New York. Oh, right, her car was currently in her driveway, home to a raccoon. Or possibly a family of bears. She'd have to settle for Amtrak.

"All right, Gia. You can do this." Sweat sprang out on her forehead, trickled down the sides of her face. This was ridiculous. She couldn't stand there staring at it all day. She inched closer. What if it was a snake?

"Hanging upside down from the bottom of a shelf? Really, Gia. Get a grip. They can't even do that, right?"

"Do what?"

Gia screamed and whirled toward the voice, swinging the makeshift weapon around with her.

Savannah held her hands in the air and scrambled back through the doorway into the hall, barley avoiding a crack on the head. "Whoa. Watch it with that thing."

Gia pressed a hand against her chest and willed her heart to slow down. "Are you crazy? What are you trying to do, scare me to death?"

Speaking of death. She whirled back toward the lump. At least it hadn't moved.

Savannah laughed. "You know, Gia, I'm actually impressed."

Gia spared her a quick glance, brow lifted.

"A year ago, you'd have run screaming from whatever it is you're stalking under there." She grinned. "Now, you're still in the same room. Granted, you're standing there talking to yourself instead of trying to get rid of it, but still. You've come a long way."

"Yeah, thanks." Although with her heart still thundering in her chest, it didn't feel like she'd made any progress at all.

"And because of that . . ." Savannah eased the pole from Gia's iron grip. "I'm going to give you a hand."

Relief rushed through her, even if Savannah did seem to be enjoying her discomfort a little too much. And even if Gia had no doubt she'd replay the entire scene for Hunt and Leo later on.

"Where?"

Gia pointed.

"What in the world?" Savannah shifted the pole to her other hand and pulled out her phone. She aimed the flashlight underneath the shelf, bent over for a closer look, then jerked upright. "Call Hunt."

"What?" Gia couldn't even imagine what was under there if Savannah needed Hunt to take care of it. And she didn't want to know. She scanned the floor around her as she high-stepped backward, just in case it didn't come alone. "My phone's in the kitchen."

Savannah shifted out of the way but kept the beam of light illuminating the object.

Emboldened when it didn't move beneath the glare, Gia moved closer. "Is that what I think it is?"

"Yup. It's a handgun taped to the underneath of the shelf."

Resigned, Gia crouched to look for any

164

other sign of tampering. "How much you wanna bet it matches the bullet they'll take out of Rusty Bragge?"

"No way I'm touching that bet." Savannah backed out of the storage closet and dialed Hunt's number. "But I'm telling you now, there's no way Cole was stupid enough to shoot Rusty, his self-proclaimed nemesis, then hide the murder weapon where he works."

Gia agreed. Unfortunately, that meant whoever did kill Rusty had been inside the café. Suddenly, the break-in made a whole lot more sense.

CHAPTER THIRTEEN

Since the crime scene techs had already gone over the café kitchen, Hunt sat at the island while Gia started on the omelet he hadn't had time for earlier, and the techs processed the storage closet.

Leo and Savannah sat across from him, fingers laced casually together.

"What did Cole say when you guys picked him up?" With one eye on the clock, since she had to open in a little more than an hour and still hadn't dropped Thor off at Zoe's doggie daycare, Gia tossed already diced ham, pepper, and onions onto the grill. Leaving Thor home with Klondike was one thing; leaving him alone all day was something else. Klondike, on the other hand, reveled in being alone. Gia had no doubt she was probably swinging from the curtains at the moment.

"About the same as he said yesterday." Hunt refilled his coffee mug for the third time since arriving. "Nothing. He didn't kill Rusty. He doesn't know who did. And he was with Cybil all morning."

Gia whirled on him, spatula raised.

He held up a hand before she could speak. "Before you ask, yes, Chief, Cybil corroborated his alibi."

"Okay, okay, sorry."

"Nah." He waved it off. "Don't be. Cole's a friend, and that's one of the things I love most about you, your sense of loyalty and willingness to go out on a limb for a friend. Even if it does occasionally drive me up a wall."

She grinned and poured the egg mixture over the ham and vegetables. "If I ever decide to give up the café, maybe I'll come to work for you."

"Over my dead body."

"I promise you I'll find your killer and bring him to justice." She shot Savannah a conspiratorial grin. "Unless it was Savannah, then I'll figure it was justifiable homicide."

Savannah hooted and slapped the counter. "You had that one coming, Hunt."

"Yeah, yeah." But the good humor faded too quickly from his eyes. "But back to Cole. He's not cooperating, and I can't figure out why."

"Do you want me to try to talk to him?" Not that she hadn't already planned to anyway.

"Yeah." He rubbed his eyes. "Maybe you can get him to open up a little more."

Gia stared at him for a moment. He must be concerned if he was willing to have Gia try to intervene. Hunt rarely, or possibly never, invited her into one of his investigations. "Is there anything I should know?"

He shook his head. "So far, we've found the receipt with Cole's name, number, and a date and time that appears to coincidentally coincide with the time of Rusty's murder, which the ME ruled was around eight a.m."

Gia latched on to *coincidentally.* Everyone knew Hunt didn't believe in coincidences any more than Gia or Savannah did.

"Then we have Rusty's business card conveniently dropped right where Cole always parks his car. And now . . ." He blew out a breath and shoved a hand through dark hair that curled past his collar and always seemed in need of a trim. "Now you just happened to stumble across a weapon taped to the bottom of a shelf Cole had access to on a regular basis on the very same morning someone broke into the café and didn't steal anything. A weapon that's been wiped, so there are no fingerprints, though I have no doubt the ballistics will match the bullet they'll pull out of Rusty when they do the autopsy later this morning. A weapon we're supposed to believe Cole hid in his place of employment after murdering someone with it."

"Not to mention the fact that Cole hasn't been back here since Rusty was found."

Hunt sat up straighter. "That's right."

Leo held up a finger. "Or a good prosecutor could argue Cole had been the one to break in, didn't want to use his key so no one would suspect he'd been here."

Savannah unlaced her fingers from his and turned a scowl on him. "You can't possibly believe that."

He shrugged. "Actually, I don't. I think someone is trying way too hard to frame him, but we still have to consider every possibility."

Savannah lowered her gaze to her coffee, her expression somber, a rare occurrence for such a happy, usually optimistic person.

Gia struggled to shut off the rapid-fire thoughts ricocheting through her head for even a few minutes as she plated omelets and home fries. The chaos in her head, along with the lack of sleep, was beginning to give her a headache. Maybe she should just call Cole and ask him if he was coming in. If so, she'd be able to talk to him, question why he was being so tight-lipped, and then take a break to get some much-needed sleep, even an hour. So much for shutting her thoughts down.

Savannah, obviously unable to sit still, jumped up to butter toast and pour orange juice.

With a quick scan of the kitchen to be sure she hadn't forgotten anything, Gia dropped onto a stool at the counter next to Hunt. "What about Caleb Ryan, the real estate guy? Were you able to get any more information on him?"

Hunt stopped with a forkful of western omelet halfway to his mouth, then lowered it to his plate. "He's a local investor, spends a lot of time and money buying up local real estate, usually renovating and then selling. We do know he was trying to get Hank's shop on Main Street, the one Rusty allegedly stole out from under him. Apparently, he's been trying to get an office open on Main Street for quite a while, but since most of the businesses along the road are owned by locals in a community that fully supports mom-and-pop shops, who pass their businesses down from one generation

170

to the next, shops don't often come available."

"And when one did, Rusty, who doesn't even live in Boggy Creek, finagled a way to get it," Leo finished.

"But is that reason enough to kill someone?" Be annoyed with them — yes. Boycott the business — for sure. Even bad-mouth them around the neighborhood. But kill?

"People have killed for less." After a quick look at his watch, Hunt finally lifted his fork and took a bite, chewed, and swallowed, then aimed a pointed look at Gia. "And before you ask, Brynleigh Colton, the woman on the zoning commission he allegedly bribed, appears to be missing in action."

"What do you mean?"

"I mean, we haven't been able to locate her. Nobody's seen her since Friday afternoon when she left work for the weekend."

"Huh. What do you think that means?"

He shrugged. "Could be anything. She's not married, lives alone, is known to travel on a whim. Although she doesn't usually miss work without calling out, her hours are flexible, and she often works from home."

"Are you concerned?"

"Let's just say I'd like to find her and have a conversation."

"Have you been able to access her bank accounts? See if she's made any large withdrawals recently?" Because if they hadn't, maybe she should reconsider Alfie's offer. Or, better yet, maybe Hunt could deputize him. At least then he wouldn't get into any trouble for hacking. She forked up home fries, took a bite while she considered her options, then realized everyone had gone silent. When she turned her attention to Hunt, she found him grinning at her. "What?"

He laughed and shook his head. "I might have to reconsider hiring you after all."

"Oh, right." Heat flamed in her cheeks. "Sorry."

"No, it's good to know if I ever forget anything, you've got my back."

She held his gaze. "Always."

His gaze lingered, and he reached out to brush a strand of hair that had come free from her ponytail behind her ear. "That goes both ways, you know."

She swallowed the lump clogging her throat and nodded. It had been a long time since she'd been able to trust anyone other than Savannah, but somewhere along the line, she'd come to trust Hunt, come to realize how much he loved her and that he'd never hurt her. At least, not intentionally.

That kind of trust didn't come easy. It was the kind you had to earn. The kind Cole had had in Rusty all those years ago, when he'd never even considered Rusty would have put the drugs into his locker. She straightened. "What about Jim Kirkman? Have you tried to find him?"

"Who?" Hunt frowned as he pulled out his notebook and shoved his nearly empty plate aside. He flipped through a few pages. "Who's Jim Kirkman? No one's mentioned him."

Gia ran through the story Cole had shared at the crime scene. "We found his wife Rhonda, who lives in Orlando and was friends with Rusty Bragge on Myspace."

Hunt paused his note-taking long enough to look up at her. "Myspace?"

"It was Alfie's idea."

He held up a finger. "Now, him I might hire."

"Ha ha." Gia stood and started to clear the island. If she didn't get moving, she'd never get open on time. Then she remembered what else Alfie had unearthed. "Alfie also said Rusty was arrested at one time for attempted murder."

Hunt's gaze flickered toward Leo for an instant, then back to Gia. "That was a sealed juvenile record."

"He didn't access it." The last thing she wanted to do was get Alfie into any kind of trouble. "He just said there was one."

"All kidding aside, I might really have to get that guy on the payroll. We're still cutting through wads of red tape trying to find out if the record even still exists or if it was expunged when he turned twenty-one." Hunt chewed on his lip, considering the pages of notes he flipped through, then stood and kissed her temple. "We've gotta go. Thank you for breakfast, and the boatload of coffee. And the tip."

She grinned at him. "Any time."

He started out of the café, then turned back to her. "Let me know if you talk to Cole."

Which she had every intention of doing before she opened. "Sure thing."

Once they were alone, Savannah started to load the dishwasher. "Why don't you go ahead and run Thor down to Zoe's while I get this cleaned up."

"You sure?"

"Yup. Everything else is done and ready to open, right?"

"Yeah." It should be, considering she'd been there all night. "I'm going to call Cole while I'm walking back."

"Let me know what he says."

"I will." Though the café would most likely be open by the time she got back, making it less likely they'd have a chance to chat until later. She grabbed her phone from the counter just as it rang and checked the caller ID, then frowned at the unfamiliar number. "Hello?"

"Hey there," the deep gravelly voice of a two-pack-a-day smoker greeted her. "This is Harvey."

"Harvey?"

"Yup, I'm out at your place. Just wanted to let you know your car's clear, and I closed the door so nothing can get back in."

The guy who'd come to relocate her raccoon. Six hundred dollars still rankled, but at least she could go home and get her car now. "Oh, that's great, thank you. You were able to catch the raccoon?"

"We-ell." His hesitation had Gia's heart sinking. "He's a smart little bugger, but I've left a trap for him, and I'll swing by a few times a day to check in."

"Is that included in the price?" Because she'd basically just paid six hundred dollars to have her car door closed. No way was she paying extra for him to keep coming back.

"Yes, ma'am. And you might want to consider keeping the garbage pails in the

175

garage."

"Okay." There was no sense being disappointed, but she was going to have to do something to keep the raccoons, and apparently bears, away. No way could she afford to throw away six hundred dollars every time a critter got into the garbage. But the thought of smelling garbage that baked in the Florida heat all day long every time she walked into the garage wasn't exactly appealing. And what if the odor seeped into the kitchen? There had to be another way. It might be less expensive to air-condition the garage than to keep calling Harvey out. "Thank you for letting me know."

"You bet."

She considered calling Cole, then decided to wait until after she'd gotten Thor to daycare. It was the only few minutes of the day she'd get to be with him, and she didn't want to spend that time on the phone, no matter how important the subject.

When she opened the front door, Earl was waiting outside. "Hey, Earl."

"Good morning."

She held the door open for him to enter. "I'm just running Thor down to daycare, then I'll be back."

"Sure thing. I just . . ." He looked up and down the road, then over his shoulder, before leaning closer to her. "Have you heard from Cole?"

"No, why?"

He shrugged and shook his head. "I've tried to call him a few times, but he's not picking up."

Gia glanced at the clock over the cutout in the dining room, then gave him an abbreviated version of the night's events.

He nodded, clutched his fisherman's cap against his chest. "Oh, well, that's a relief then."

"A relief?"

"If Hunt and Leo took him into the station, that would explain why he's not answering his door either."

Gia stilled, the urgency of getting Thor to daycare and back in time to open the café suddenly less important. "Hunt and Leo stopped by his house to question him. As far as I know, they didn't ask him to go to the station."

"Oh." Earl paled.

"When did you go by his house?"

"On my way here." He checked the time on his cell phone. "About twenty minutes ago."

"Okay. All right. Let me get Thor taken care of, and we'll figure out what's going on." Where would he have gone? She really hoped he hadn't decided to skip town, but if he did, she had to find him before anyone else realized he was missing. And she'd better find him quickly, in case something had happened to him and he actually did need the police.

CHAPTER FOURTEEN

After walking Thor to daycare, and receiving assurances from Zoe that she always had room for Thor and that Trevor would be dropping his German shepherd, Brandy, off to play with him in a few hours, Gia started back down Main Street at a brisk pace. She tried Cole's number, to no avail, then shoved the phone back into the pocket of her leggings.

As she passed the shop that would have housed Rusty's new deli, the one he'd planned to use to put her out of business, she slowed. With a quick look around to be sure she wouldn't be observed and become the talk of the town, Gia peered inside the darkened interior. Even using her hand to shield the glare of the sun, she couldn't make out anything more than shapes and shadows, none of them human, inside the building. Frustrated, she gave up and tried Cole's number again. Straight to voicemail.

Either he'd turned the phone off or he'd ghosted her. Either way, it was obvious he didn't want to be bothered. That being the case, she gave up and dialed Cybil's number, then cringed when she remembered how early it was but didn't hang up.

"Hello, Gia." At least it didn't sound like she'd just been awakened by the phone.

"Hi, Cybil. I'm so sorry to bother you this early."

"Don't worry about it, I was just heading out to walk Caesar."

"Do you think that's a good idea with a killer on the loose?" Gia had never liked the idea of Cybil wandering the woods alone, but Cybil had insisted she'd been doing so for most of her life and wasn't about to give up the habit. While Gia had felt better about it once Cybil had adopted Caesar, now that someone had been murdered in the forest, she wished Cybil would stick close to home.

Cybil sighed, and Gia had no doubt she knew exactly where Gia's thoughts had strayed, an uncanny ability that had made Gia think the woman was psychic the first time they'd met. "We're just walking in the neighborhood for now."

"That's probably a good idea. At least until Hunt figures out who killed Rusty." As far as segues went, it was about as good as she was going to get. "Speaking of . . ."

Cybil chuckled softly. "I figured that's why you were calling so early. Just give me a minute to get out."

"Sure." Gia held on, listening to the sound of muffled voices followed by a loud bang before Cybil returned.

"Okay, sorry, I just wanted to get outside so we could talk privately."

"Privately? Who's there?" Since Cybil lived alone . . .

"He's here, Gia," she said softly.

"Cole? What's he doi . . . oh . . . uh . . ." Talk about dense. Heat flared in her cheeks. "I'm so sorry, Cybil. I didn't mean to intrude."

"Don't worry about it, and it's not what you think." Gia could practically hear her grin. "Although it might be some of that too."

Ah, man. She did not need to know that. Now she felt even worse for calling so early and interrupting. "I'm really sorry, Cybil. One of these days, I'll learn to mind my own business."

"I certainly hope not. Then you'd be a bore." She laughed out loud. "I'm just messing with you, Gia. Cole came over and stayed last night, on the couch, because he didn't want me to be alone after, well, finding Rusty and all, but he had to turn his phone off because it rang nonstop half the night."

A million questions raged through her head, demanding answers, but only one mattered at the moment. "Is he okay?"

"To be honest, I'm not sure. That's why I wanted to talk to you alone." She paused, the hesitation unusual for the normally confident woman. "He's not acting like himself."

"What do you mean?"

"He's quiet, sullen. After your run-in with Rusty and Amanda in the café, he came to talk to me. He told me what happened with him and Amanda —"

"What happened between them?" she blurted before she could restrain herself, her curiosity getting the better of her.

"Sorry, sweetie, but that's Cole's story to tell."

"You're right." No matter how disappointed she was she'd have to wait for answers, those answers should come from Cole. "I'm sorry."

"No worries. You're just concerned. As am I."

"Cybil, do you know why he's not cooperating more with the investigation?"

"I don't. And that's part of what has me

so concerned. Hang on."

Gia listened in the background just in case Cybil needed help. This murder really had her spooked.

She returned a moment later. "That was Cole. He wanted to let me know he's going into work this morning."

Gia breathed a sigh of relief. Maybe getting back to his daily routine would help. Plus, now she'd have the opportunity to question him herself, gauge what was going on, and maybe figure out a way to help him.

"Do me a favor, and let me know if there's anything you think he needs from me?" Cybil asked. "I'm not used to feeling so helpless."

"Of course, Cybil. Thank you." And it occurred to her that Cybil had never once asked if Cole might have confided anything in Gia, only what she could do to help him. The realization that Cybil had fallen in love with Cole struck with sudden clarity, and her heart ached for the couple. "I'll let you know anything I find out."

"Thanks, I appreciate that. And I don't know if he'll say it to you or not, but I want you to know how much he appreciates you standing by him and believing in him."

"Of course. We'll get this straightened out, Cybil, but it would be a whole lot easier if he would open up and talk to the police more."

"I know. I'm working on it."

Knowing it was the best she could ask for, Gia hung up and stuffed the phone into her pocket. She unlocked the café door, then left it open as she hurried inside. It was only five minutes until opening time anyway. Earl was seated at the counter with a cup of coffee, and a handful of customers already stood on the sidewalk waiting.

Unfortunately, with Cole still absent, Gia spent the morning rush in front of the grill with little time to think or talk to anyone. As one of Boggy Creek's growing gossip hot spots, the café thrived on mornings when gossip flew. She just wished business would be as robust without anyone being killed.

She checked the row of tickets, drizzled a line of oil, and cracked half a dozen eggs onto the grill. From a bin already heating on the back of the grill, she grabbed bacon and sausage and set it beside the eggs to warm it further. With that cooking, she cut and dropped three kaiser rolls into toasters, spooned home fries onto two of the plates and grits into a bowl, added salt and pepper to all three rolls and a swirl of ketchup to one.

She never did understand the appeal of

ketchup on egg sandwiches, but an awful lot of people loved it, so she figured there had to be something to it.

The sizzle of eggs frying, the scent of breakfast meat and coffee, and the sound of people chatting drifting through the cutout from the dining room brought a smile. The homey atmosphere was exactly what she'd envisioned when she'd first had the idea for the café. After piling the eggs, meat, and cheese onto the rolls, she ladled pancake batter onto the grill for the next order and shoved the three plates onto the cutout for Savannah or Willow to pick up.

A quick glance into the dining room showed a full house, every seat taken, every counter stool filled, and a few people waiting for seats. The Bailey sisters sat smack in the middle of the chaos. If their grins were any indication, rumors were most definitely flying. She just hoped none of them involved Cole as a killer. A quick glance at the clock showed he was already an hour late. Maybe Cybil had been wrong, or maybe he'd changed his mind about coming in.

The smell of burning batter yanked her from thoughts better left alone while she was trying to cook. She quickly scraped the burnt pancakes from the grill and started over. With the dining room packed and more customers waiting, she had to get her head in the game.

The kitchen door swung open. "Gia?"

She didn't turn at the sound of Savannah's voice, couldn't lest she lose track of what she was doing. "What's up?"

"There's a woman out front insisting she needs to speak with you. She says it's urgent."

A flashback of Rusty's rant shot through her head. The last thing she needed right now, especially with how crowded they were, was an irate customer. "Was she unhappy with something?"

"No. Actually, she didn't even order anything. She just came in and said she wanted to speak with the owner."

"Great," she muttered as she plated the pancakes, added them to a tray with butter, syrup, and powdered sugar. "There's no way I can get out front right now. Did you ask her what she wants?"

"Yes, and she wouldn't tell me, just that it was imperative that she speak with you about an urgent matter. And Gia?"

She spared her a quick glance as she set the tray on the cutout.

"It seemed like she's been crying."

Gia paused. "You think it has something to do with Rusty's murder?"

"I don't know." Savannah glanced toward the dining room. "But I have a feeling we shouldn't just dismiss her and send her on her way."

"Okay. All right." No way could she leave the grill. Even if she could pull Savannah from the floor to cover the back for a few minutes, it would leave Willow waiting tables alone. No matter how good she was, she couldn't handle a packed house on her own. "Get her coffee or something, and bring her back here. I'll talk to her while I'm cooking. And if that's not good for her, she'll have to come back later on when we're not as busy."

"You bet." She rapped her knuckles against the door once, then let it swing shut as she hurried back out to the front.

Gia yanked the orders she'd completed off the grill and slid the next five down. Though she couldn't help being curious about her visitor, it really wasn't the best time to entertain her.

Savannah shoved the door open again and ushered a tall, thin but curvy woman into the kitchen, then set a coffee mug on the center island. "Here you go, hon. This here's Gia."

"Hello, Gia." The woman's voice held a bit of a twang. "Thank you so much for

187

agreeing to see me. I know how busy you are."

"No problem." Savannah was right — the woman did appear upset. Tears shimmered in big blue eyes that were already red-rimmed and puffy from crying. It didn't escape Gia's notice that Savannah hadn't introduced the woman, which meant she didn't know her name — and considering her impeccable Southern manners and charm, she most definitely would have asked. Curiouser and curiouser.

Savannah pulled out a stool for her. "You can sit and have your coffee while Gia works, and if you need anything, you just give a holler."

The woman made no move to sit. "Thank you again for your kindness."

"Of course." And then Savannah was gone, leaving Gia alone with the stranger.

"So, how can I help you, Ms. . . . uh . . ."

"Ariyah." Leaving her coffee untouched on the counter, the woman peered through the cutout and scanned the dining room, then turned to face Gia. Wrapping her arms around herself, she leaned back against the counter. "I'm Ariyah O'Neil."

"It's nice to meet you, Ariyah. How can I help you?"

"I'm not sure." She caught her lower lip

188

between her teeth, glanced into the dining room again, then inched closer to Gia and lowered her voice. "I saw you talking to Amanda Bragge yesterday morning."

Gia ran through the interaction at the hotel. The only person she'd seen in the hallway, other than Amanda, had been Caleb Ryan. A niggle of unease crept up her spine and settled at the base of her neck.

"I saw you go into her room, and I recognized you from the picture Rusty showed me on the computer."

"Wait." She fumbled a plate, thankfully empty, and it crashed to the floor. Great. She stripped off her gloves and grabbed the broom and dustpan. "You knew Rusty?"

She nodded, chewing so hard on her lower lip Gia expected her to gnaw a hole right through it. "He and I were . . ."

Tears spilled over, running down her cheeks. She lowered her face into her hands, quietly sobbing.

The fact that Rusty would have been looking at pictures of Gia, online or anywhere else, upped the creep factor tremendously. Giving Ariyah a moment to collect herself, Gia finished cleaning up the shattered plate then dropped a stack of napkins on the counter and washed her hands. "Look, Ariyah, if you want to talk to me, you're going to have to be a little more forthcoming."

"Okay." She swallowed hard, lowered her voice to a whisper. "I think I know who killed Rusty, and I'm afraid I'm going to be next."

CHAPTER FIFTEEN

Gia's mouth fell open, and she snapped it closed again. Her heart rate ratcheted up. Could Ariyah really know who the killer was? What if she was right, and the killer planned to target her next? What if she'd been followed? What if everyone in the building was in danger? Her employees? Her customers? Gia glanced out into the dining room. Not to mention the fact that any one of the customers out there could be a killer.

She dismissed the thought. If she started thinking like that, she may as well give up everything and stay home. Since she had no intention of doing that, it was probably best to figure out who the killer was. Or, at least, who Ariyah thought the killer was.

Willow poked her head through the cutout. "Hey, Gia, what's the holdup?"

"Oh, right, sorry." She shook off the momentary shock. "I dropped a dish, but it's cleaned up now, and I'll get everything out in a hurry. Just apologize and take ten percent off all of the bills until I get caught up."

"Sure thing, but hurry up." She plastered on a smile and turned to face the masses.

Gia had no doubt she and Savannah would take care of the front, but she had to get moving. With her head reeling, she scanned the tickets and set out to catch up. She glanced over her shoulder then gestured for Ariyah to move closer. "Who do you think the killer is?"

"His wife, that witch." She rubbed at her already blotchy face, turning her cheeks raw. "She couldn't stand the fact that Rusty and me were together."

Whoa. Wait. That was new. "You were having an affair?"

"Uh-huh." She nodded and sniffed.

If Amanda knew about the affair, and it had been motive enough for her to kill him, it certainly would explain her blasé attitude about his death. "How did you see me going into Amanda's room?"

"I'm staying in the room across the hall from her."

"Across . . ." So, Rusty had his wife in one room and his mistress holed up across the hall? What kind of man did that?

"Well, technically, Rusty's room was right

across the hall from Amanda's, but Rusty and I had a connecting door, and I was looking through Rusty's peephole waiting for him to come back when that man, Caleb, started yelling at Amanda, and then you showed up."

Gia figured she was watching to see if Rusty returned to Amanda's room instead of his own, but she didn't bother calling her on it. Whatever her reasons for watching Amanda's room didn't matter in the grand scheme of things. At least, not that Gia could see, but that would be up to the police to decide. "Have you gone to the police?"

She shook her head, eyes wide.

"Why not?"

"Because I can't prove anything, but before he left to go meet up with Cole —"

"Wait." Gia held up the spatula she'd been about to flip a line of eggs with. "He was going to meet Cole?"

"Yes."

"You're sure of that?" Maybe directing her to the police wasn't the best idea.

She pursed her lips, then dropped her gaze to the floor. "It's where he said he was going, but I guess he could have lied."

"Did he do that often? Lie?"

She nodded.

"But you stayed with him anyway?"

She lifted a shoulder, let it fall. "You have to understand men like Rusty. They are always searching for something more, never satisfied to just accept their lot in life. That's what makes them so successful in business."

She had to wonder if this woman had any clue that Rusty's money came from his wife rather than any successful business ventures.

"I was willing to accept that. I knew Rusty loved me. He only stayed with his wife for the money."

Well, that shot that theory. Perhaps she was nothing more than a gold digger, and it didn't matter to her where his money came from.

"And as far as the zoning woman, he only slept with her to get the permits and whatnot he needed to open a deli."

"Wait, he was sleeping with someone on the zoning board too?" And Brynleigh was the only woman on the board. Brynleigh, who'd been accused of accepting bribes, who'd disappeared right after, or perhaps before, Rusty's death.

"Yeah, but it's not like he cared about her or anything."

Gia lifted a hand to massage her throbbing temples, then remembered she was working grill and lowered her hand. As soon as things calmed down, she'd get herself a couple of ibuprofen, but for now . . .

She slid two more orders onto the cutout. Somehow, she needed to sort through Ariyah's revelations and figure out what was important. "Okay, you said Rusty told you he was headed out to meet Cole. When was that?"

"Around five o'clock Monday morning."

"Five?" The time on the card had said eight. "Why so early?"

"I don't know. He just said that was where he was going. He'd already taken care of Jim, and he just had to deal with Cole before he and I could run off together and get married."

It felt like a hot knife poking behind her eyes. "Taken care of Jim?"

"That's right. Cole was the last person left who'd ever bested him, and he was determined to have his revenge. After that, he was going to tell Amanda he wanted a divorce, and that's why she killed him."

Gia shook her head, trying to understand how this woman thought anything about that scenario was okay. "If Amanda was the one with the money, why would she kill him for divorcing her? It's not like she needed the inheritance."

Quite honestly, Gia didn't think Amanda would care one way or the other, considering she'd outright admitted she despised the man. Especially if Savannah's suspicions about her and Caleb having an affair were true.

"Because she didn't want to pay him alimony, of course." Ariyah narrowed one eye at Gia, tilted her head. "Haven't you been paying attention?"

"Apparently not as well as I should be." Two tickets left, and unless Savannah or Willow charged in with more, she might get a break. She tossed vegetables onto the grill, cracked three eggs into a stainless-steel bowl, and tried to figure out how this conversation helped Cole. Actually, it didn't. If Ariyah was right, and Rusty had gone to meet Cole, it looked even worse.

It didn't matter. Cole hadn't killed anyone, and the truth of that would come out either way. "Ariyah, you need to go to the police and talk to them. If Amanda did kill Rusty, what makes you think she'll come after you next?"

"Because I saw her leave the hotel about ten minutes after he did, and she saw me looking out the window."

"Okay. You need to talk to the police and tell them what you've told me. If you want, I can call Captain Hunt and have him meet you here."

She was already shaking her head as she stood from where she'd leaned a hip against the counter. "No. I'll go to the police station and talk to them."

While Gia didn't like the idea of sending the woman out on her own if someone really did want to kill her, she couldn't force her to stay. "Go straight to the station and ask for Captain Quinn or Detective Dumont, okay?"

"I will. I want that woman behind bars for what she did to my poor Rusty, and I hope they throw away the key." She flounced toward the door, swung it open, then paused and looked back over her shoulder. She sucked in a deep, shuddering breath. "I know you probably don't understand it, but I loved him, even knowing what he was like. And she took him from me. I suppose the last thing I can do for my honey bear now is to see he gets justice."

As far as dramatic exits went, it wasn't the best she'd ever seen. And it was way too contrived, as if she'd practiced the parting words until she'd gotten them just right, her expression perfect so she looked beautiful, courageous, and determined. Too bad she wasn't a good enough actress to pull it off. Because, despite a heroic effort, she couldn't hide the cold calculation in those baby blues.

Savannah strode through the door just as Gia was putting up the last order and set two full coffee mugs on the counter. "Well, what was that all about?"

Gia set the order on the cutout for Willow. The café had cleared out a little, and it seemed the remaining customers were either eating or nursing coffees. She emptied Ariyah's untouched coffee into the sink and put the mug in the dishwasher, then sat across from Savannah at the island. Her feet ached the moment she got off them.

Knowing the momentary lull could end at any moment, Gia gave Savannah a quick rundown of Ariyah's accusations. "Honestly, I'm not quite sure what she's trying to say. It seems like she was trying to sell Amanda as Rusty's killer, but at the same time she said Rusty told her he was going to meet Cole, which doesn't look good for him, since he didn't admit to arranging a meeting."

"But she said she saw Amanda leaving right after Rusty did?"

And she had seen Gia go to Amanda's room, so she apparently did have a view of Amanda's door. "Yeah, and that Amanda saw her looking out the window. There's only one problem with that."

"What's that?"

"Think about it. If Ariyah and Rusty's rooms were across the hall from Amanda's —"

Savannah snapped her fingers. "She wouldn't have had a view of the parking lot. And the valet area is covered, so she wouldn't have seen her there either. So, little miss sweet and innocent wasn't where she said she was."

"Exactly."

"Do you think Ariyah killed him?" Savannah frowned. "If so, what's her motive?"

"Who knows? A woman scorned, maybe?"

Savannah tapped her nails against her mug. "If that's the motive you're looking at, seems it could easily have been Ariyah or Amanda."

"Or Brynleigh, who Ariyah swears was also having an affair with Rusty."

"Yet Caleb said he bribed her." Savannah shook her head. "For a man who treated everyone so poorly, he had an awful lot of women interested."

"Go figure." But the person most on Gia's mind was Jim Kirkman, who Ariyah had admitted Rusty had done something to. "Speaking of women, I really need to track down Rhonda Kirkman and see what she has to say."

"Sounds like a plan." Savannah stood. "We can go after work if you want. We can take Thor with us, then I'll drop you guys off home after."

"Hey, Gia." Alfie poked his head through the cutout from the dining room. "You got a sec?"

"Yeah, sure, come on back."

He glanced at Savannah, then back to Gia. "It would be better if we spoke somewhere a little more private."

Excitement coursed through her, along with dread. He'd found something, but in the middle of the café, even with the morning rush subsiding, privacy would be hard to come by.

"Go ahead and take him into your office. I can cover the grill for a bit, and if we get another rush, I'll knock on the door," Savannah offered.

"You're sure?"

"Yup. And if you don't get to fill me in before we leave, you can do so on the way over to Rhonda's."

Gia stood, suddenly eager to see what Alfie might have unearthed. "Thanks, Savannah."

"Sure."

Gia took her coffee with her and met Alfie by her office door, then waited for him to

200

precede her. By the time she'd shut the door and crossed the room to sit with her coffee, Alfie had already claimed her desk chair and was setting up his laptop.

Gia sat across from him and sipped her coffee, then tilted her head back and closed her eyes. Just for a minute. She drifted somewhere between wakefulness and sleep until her hand loosened a bit too much and coffee tipped over the rim of her mug, jerking her back awake.

Alfie paused, cord half plugged in, to stare at her. "You okay?"

"Yeah, sorry. I didn't get any sleep last night."

"Why not?" He finished setting up, sat, and flexed his fingers.

She'd forgotten he wouldn't have heard about the night's events. "Someone broke into the café last night."

"Oh, no." He barely spared her a glance. "Did they steal much?"

"Nothing, actually." She gave him a quick recap, ending with finding the gun she was a hundred and ten percent sure would turn out to be the murder weapon.

"Wow. Huh." Alfie was not known to be a man of few words, so the fact that he simply returned to whatever he was doing without grilling her further piqued her curiosity.

"So, what did you find?"

"Okay, let me start by saying, what I tell you in this room stays between us."

"Right." She assumed he understood she'd share with Savannah, since everyone knew she shared everything with Savannah. But she should probably make sure since he seemed so serious. "I can tell Savannah, right?"

"Oh, yeah, sure, but she can't tell Leo, and you can't tell Hunt."

Uh-oh. There she was, straddling that thin line again, trying to balance loyalty to her friends with honesty to Hunt. "Um."

He waved her off. "Listen, if what I found turns out to be important, I'll find a way to drop him an anonymous tip, but for now, I wouldn't want to have to explain."

Everything in her stilled. "Explain what?"

He winced. "Explain how I might have — probably not exactly legally — hacked into several local security and traffic cameras and came up with pieced-together footage of certain individuals in the vicinity of or entering the Ocala National Forest early on the same morning Rusty Bragge was found dead."

CHAPTER SIXTEEN

Eagerness for answers warred with integrity as Gia contemplated accessing the information Alfie had found. She could just say no, thank him, and forget he'd said anything. But if he'd found something that might exonerate Cole, how could she ignore it? She couldn't. Okay, so then what? Surely Hunt and Leo could, and probably already did, have some kind of cyber-whiz at the department combing through the same footage.

Alfie's finger hovered over the keyboard. "Yes or no?"

Ignoring the angel on her shoulder, she nodded. "Do it."

If nothing came of it, she didn't have to say anything. If they learned something important, well, like Alfie said, there was always the good old anonymous tip. Or just being honest with her fiancé, which was the more difficult path but the one she'd follow.

Alfie saved her any further internal struggle when he spun the computer toward her, rounded the desk to stand over her shoulder, and hit the Enter key. A map of the Ocala National Forest and the surrounding areas popped up. "Now, keep in mind, there are two main public forest entrances that make sense to use if you're coming from Boggy Creek, which is on the south side of the forest."

To orient herself, she quickly found the area where the café was located, then traced the path to her house on the outskirts of the forest. "Okay."

"To access the park somewhere else, you'd have to either go around or head straight through the forest, which means you'd still have to come up from the south on one of these two roads." He traced a finger along the only main road that cut through the forest, then tapped a spot to the east along the Ocklawaha River. "This is where Rusty was found, so it would be an awfully far walk from this road to the riverbank. Even if someone was looking for a clandestine meeting, it seems like quite a hike."

"Yes, it does. And we don't even know yet if Rusty was killed where he was found." Even if you assumed for a fraction of a second that Cole was guilty, there was no way he could have carried Rusty that distance through the woods. Hopefully, Hunt would realize that too. Unless, of course, Cole had an accomplice. So who was in the forest that might be loyal enough to Cole to help him? Cybil, who was supposedly with him when he found Rusty's body. And Harley — her stomach pitched — who was washing his hands in the river when she'd seen him. She shook off the thoughts. Focusing on who didn't kill Rusty wasn't going to help Cole. They needed to figure out who did.

Alfie had a new tab open with video footage of a dirt parking lot and a spattering of bugs and moths hovering around the light.

Gia squinted to bring the background into better focus.

"There are not a lot of businesses in the area, but this here's the camera from the bar a little over two miles from the south forest entrance closest to where Rusty was found."

"Hey, I know that place." Gia sometimes passed the small, no-frills local bar on her way home from work when she felt like taking the scenic route. Though, she'd never seen more than a handful of cars in the lot and wouldn't have expected them to have security cameras in the parking lot.

"The cameras cover the lot and the road out front, and if you watch right here . . ." He moved the cursor to the top of the screen and waited, then hit Pause when a car came into the shot. "That's Rusty's car. Check the time stamp. Six-oh-seven."

"How can you be sure it's Rusty's?"

"License plate."

"Huh." She didn't bother asking — plausible deniability and all that. Besides, there was a much bigger question to be answered. "What was he doing there so early? If the time on the back of the receipt Officer Erickson found is accurate, the meet with Cole wasn't supposed to be for almost two hours. It wouldn't have taken more than fifteen minutes or so to walk from that parking lot to the spot he was found."

"Hold that thought." He grabbed a Post-it pad from her desk and a pen from the cupholder on the corner and jotted down *6:07 a.m. — Rusty — Camera 1,* then switched to a new tab.

While she waited, she brought up a map of the area in her mind. Between the bar and the nearest public forest entrance there were only trees, a sprinkling of rural homes, a farm, and one mom-and-pop gas station/ grocery store, not the kind of place Rusty would have lounged over a leisurely breakfast, which begged the question, what was he doing there so early?

"See here." Alfie positioned the cursor near the clock running in the bottom corner. "Two minutes later, another car passes."

Gia squinted when he paused the footage, barely able to make out a silhouette in the passenger seat. "Who's that?"

"Ariyah O'Neil, or at least, it's a car registered in her name."

"Close enough to be following him but hanging back so he wouldn't see her?" Had his mistress killed him? She was the first person Gia had come across who'd seemed genuinely upset by his death. Could it all have been an act? Had Gia mistaken regret for grief? Maybe she'd killed him in the heat of the moment?

Alfie added *6:09 — Ariyah O'Neil — Camera 1,* then switched to a new tab.

"Hey, wait, I was still —"

"Hang on. I'll leave all the tabs open, but let me lay it all out first." He pulled up another camera. Gia recognized the gas station/bait shop just before the forest entrance. "That's right by the entrance Trevor and I came in."

"Yup. You guys pass the camera a few minutes before eight."

Right around the time Cole and Rusty

207

were supposedly meeting. A thought intruded. If Rusty was in the forest as early as a little past six, he could have already been dead when Cole arrived to meet him. Maybe that's why Cole was so quiet. Maybe he was just afraid to admit he'd been planning to meet up with him.

He paused the camera footage as a pickup truck pulled out and wrote *4:45 a.m. — Officer Erickson — Camera 2.* "I'm assuming he stopped for gas or coffee on his way into work, probably for a shift that started at five."

"You don't think he had anything to do with Rusty's death, do you?" Because he was the first one to approach the body, and that would throw into question whether or not he'd actually found the receipt on Rusty or had planted it. Or that could be wishful thinking.

"No. I have no reason to suspect they even knew each other. Plus, he entered the forest farther south." He fast-forwarded through the footage. "I'm just trying to put as many people who were present at the scene in place as I can."

A car sped through the scene, and Gia grabbed Alfie's wrist. "Wait. Who was that?"

He shook his head. "There are a few other cars that go through, but some I've already eliminated as people who live in the area, campers, or people who visit the forest regularly. The list would be too long to go through everyone who passed by, but I do have them all documented if we need them later. I would have excluded Erickson on my initial sweep too, except it seemed prudent to include him since he was on the scene."

"Okay." They could always comb through the footage again or go through Alfie's notes if they didn't come up with any viable suspects.

He hit Pause when the counter read seven twenty-seven. "And here we have Amanda Bragge passing by, moving at a pretty fast clip, too."

"But she's entering a different lot, an hour and a half after Rusty went in, so she wasn't following him."

"Nope, but she could have known where he was going and when."

"True." So, now they had Ariyah and Amanda both in the area at the time of his death. A conspiracy? Did Ariyah get tired of Rusty cheating on her? Upset that he wouldn't divorce his wife? But Ariyah had insisted Amanda had killed him. Had she seen Amanda in the forest that morning? Maybe even seen her murder him?

"And this SUV belongs to Rusty's competition, in both business and love, if Savannah's instincts are spot on."

Which they usually were.

He jotted down *7:28 — Amanda Bragge — Camera 2,* and *7:33 — Caleb Ryan — Camera 2,* then set the video in motion again and paused it a moment later when a white sedan rolled onto the screen. "And this here, I'm only including because I was unable to find any information on the vehicle other than that it was rented at the Orlando Airport on the day before the murder."

"You couldn't find who rented it?"

He frowned and shook his head slowly. "It's rented to a corporation, not an individual, and I couldn't find a record of who exactly picked it up. The best I could try to do is match an incoming flight to the time of the rental, but Orlando is a huge international airport. Something like that would take time, and it would help to have an idea who we were looking at or where the flight might have originated. Realistically, it's probably just a family from the Midwest or a businessman from up north driving a scenic route from one place to another."

She nodded, distracted. "We already have Rusty, Ariyah, Amanda, Caleb, and Wade Erickson in the forest at the time of the murder, so we don't need to focus on a stranger just yet, but the one person I didn't see going in is Cole."

"I assume he and Cybil walked in, if they'd been staying at her house."

"Hmm. That's true. And we already know Harley would have walked."

"Right, and I forgot to add Donna Mae to the list, though her car passes Camera 1 at the bar at around eight as well." He added her name and info to the list and pulled up the footage of her driving past the bar alone.

"Okay, now." He pointed to Donna Mae. "We are assuming for the moment that everyone entering the forest that day had been driving their own cars."

She nodded. It was a big assumption, but they weren't detectives, so they could take the leap. For now, anyway.

"But, if you look closely, you can tell for sure Donna Mae is driving her car and alone."

"Okay."

He switched to the same camera when Ariyah passed by. "Again, you can tell she's the only one in the car."

"Yes."

"But look here." He switched to Rusty's tab. "Granted, Donna Mae and Ariyah are both driving cars, and Rusty is driving an

211

SUV, so the angles are different, but look at this shadow."

Rusty was visible in the driver's seat, but the passenger seat was shrouded in shadow. In spite of that, you could kind of make out the silhouette of a second person. "Someone was in the car with him?"

Alfie only shrugged. "It was raining at the time, so it could be a reflection, an optical illusion, a shadow cast by the streetlights or even the sun beginning to rise, or . . ."

"Or it could be Rusty wasn't alone when he went into that forest." Suddenly the fact that they couldn't place Cole driving into the forest took on a much more ominous feel.

CHAPTER SEVENTEEN

Gia tossed the players around in her mind while she hustled her way through the busier than usual lunch rush. When the door swung open, she didn't bother to look up.

"Hey, there."

She whirled to find Cole standing in the doorway, a baseball cap clutched in his hands. She ran to him, gave him a quick hug, and returned to the grill. "Hey. Where have you been?"

"I'm sorry." He hung the hat on a hook, then went to the sink to wash his hands. "I didn't mean to leave you stuck."

"Oh, man, Cole. I don't care about that. I've just been crazy worried about you." She flipped six pancakes, dipped three slices of French bread into batter, and tossed them onto the grill.

He paused, hands full of suds. "It's okay with you if I come in to work, right?"

"Of course it is. Why wouldn't it be?" A

quick glance at the next ticket.

He shrugged and finished washing up, then donned gloves. "I just don't want the café's reputation to be tarnished because I'm being investigated. If you think it would be better for me to wait until I'm cleared to come back, I'd understand."

"Cole, do you know how many people have dropped in to say they support you and know you didn't have anything to do with Rusty's murder?" Because she'd lost count.

His cheeks flamed red, and he averted his gaze to study the row of tickets still lined along the grill. "Savannah, Willow, and Skyla all said."

"So, no more talk of not working. I need you." She flipped the French toast, plated the pancakes.

He nodded. "You want grill or prep?"

She plated two omelets, the order of French toast, and a side of grits, then set them all on the cutout. Using the back of her wrist, she swiped back a few free strands of hair that had escaped her ponytail and fallen into her face. "I could use a break from the heat, if you're up to it."

"You bet I am." He grinned as he gave her a two-finger salute and took the spatula from her. "Honestly, I could use the distraction."

Gia brought him up to speed on where she was, then grabbed a bottle of water from the fridge and held it up. "You want?"

"Nah." He studied the next ticket, started cracking eggs onto the grill. "I'm good, thanks."

She opened the water and sucked down half the bottle. Even in the air-conditioned café, working in front of the grill all day was rough. Maybe she'd get used to it after a few more sweltering Florida summers. She set the water aside and took a moment to smooth her hair back and wash her hands. As much as she wanted to dive right in, interrogate Cole, and share what she, Savannah, and Alfie had found so far, she waited, giving him a chance to get his bearings.

Donning new gloves, she fell into their usual easy rhythm. But the tension proved too much. She had to have answers. "Cole . . ."

He closed his eyes for a moment, then opened them and met her gaze. "Yeah."

The weariness she saw there stilled her questions. "I won't pry. I just want you to know I'm here if you need to talk. Or if there's anything you need."

"Thanks, Gia. I can't tell you how much I

appreciate that."

She nodded and checked the next ticket. Pancakes and a southwestern omelet. Since Cole hadn't yet poured the eggs for the omelet, she dropped two slices of rye bread into a toaster but didn't push it down. Instead, she poured a cup of syrup and added it to a plate, then added a side of butter and another of powdered sugar. Then she popped the bread down, checked the next ticket, and measured what was needed against Cole's progress on the grill.

Usually, she could barely keep up with him. He could move faster on a grill than anyone she'd ever worked with. But today he seemed slow, a bit more sluggish than she'd ever seen him. Still, she bit her tongue. Let him move at his own pace. Let him talk when he was ready.

"Would you mind not thinking so loud?" Cole winked. "It's starting to give me a headache."

"Sorry."

He chuckled and shook his head. "No worries. I appreciate the effort. Honestly, I took a long walk before coming in to clear my head, and I was going to talk to you as soon as I got here, but you made such a valiant effort not to intrude, I didn't want it to be wasted."

The knot of tension in her gut eased. "Well, thanks for that. I appreciate it, but if you're done being noble now, could you please tell me what's going on?"

He sighed as he ran down the line of tickets, the work second nature and an odd sort of comfort when you were dealing with something difficult. A feeling Gia knew well. "I don't even know where to start."

"Why don't you start with Amanda?" Since she seemed to be the main catalyst that had upset Cole so badly when Rusty had come into the café, despite all the rude and insulting things he'd said to Cole.

"Amanda was the love of my life." He jerked his head to make eye contact with Gia. "Was. Past tense. Now, well . . ."

He returned his attention to the grill, but not before she caught the flash of pain in his eyes.

"What?"

He tapped the spatula against the front of the grill a few times, flipped it in his hand, caught it. When some part of him won whatever internal battle he'd been waging, his shoulders slumped. "I'm going to tell you something, but I need an assurance from you that it won't leave this room. You can't tell Hunt. You can't even tell Savannah."

Uh-oh. Did she trust Cole enough to make that promise? What could be so awful he wouldn't want anyone else to know about it? Unless he confessed to murder, which she had no doubt he wouldn't, it wasn't up to her to repeat anything he said in confidence. And if he did confess to murder, well, she'd deal with that if the time came. "Okay."

He tilted his head, lifted a brow. "That's it? Okay."

"Yup." Laying a hand on his arm, she waited for him to look at her. "Whatever's going on, Cole, I trust you, I believe in you, and I will do whatever I can to help."

He nodded. "Thank you for that. For everything."

"Of course." But despite the importance of whatever discussion they were about to have, they would have to pick up the pace or they'd fall behind. As it was, things were moving slower than they needed to. Gia grabbed the pancake batter, slid beside Cole in front of the grill, and started ladling batter. "Talk to me, Cole. I promise everything will stay between us."

Hopefully, she wouldn't live to regret that promise.

"No one knows this yet, not even Cybil, but . . ." He blew out a breath. "I was going to propose."

Shock held her tongue. Whatever confession she'd been expecting, that hadn't even been on her radar.

"Are you going to say something?"

"Oh, uh, I'm sorry. You just caught me by surprise. I didn't even have a clue you two were dating, though I started to suspect it after Cybil said you'd spent the night." Some detective she was. "But that's awesome. You know how I feel about you, and Cybil is amazing. I think you guys make a great couple."

"Did."

She frowned. "What do you mean? Cybil broke up with you?"

"No. I broke up with her."

"Why would you do that?" She ran through the phone call with Cybil — no mention of any tension between them, though she'd never exactly admitted they were seeing each other either. "When did you break up with her?"

"This morning before I left."

She had no way to know if he'd broken up with her before or after Gia had spoken to her. She'd have to call her later and make sure she was okay. "Why?"

"Because none of this is fair to her."

"Okay." She could certainly understand

wanting to protect someone you loved. Had that been why he'd broken things off with Amanda? "Okay, let's leave that alone for a minute. Actually, scratch that. I can't. Let me just say Cybil has been nothing but worried about you. I've spoken to her a couple of times since Rusty was found, and her only concern seemed to be how to protect you, support you, and if you were okay. So, what really doesn't seem fair is that you don't have enough faith in her to know she can handle this and stand by the person she loves. There. That's all I'll say."

"Ouch."

"Well, sometimes the truth hurts." Honestly, so far, everyone had indulged Cole in feeling sorry for himself. While she certainly understood the urge to do so, when Gia had been the one having a pity party, Savannah had given her a good swift kick in the bottom. Not that she could tell Cole to pull up his big girl pants, but it was time to stop tiptoeing around him and coddling. "What happened with Amanda?"

"We were supposed to get married, and a few days before the wedding, I walked in and found her in Rusty's arms." His jaw clenched. "And it was far from platonic."

She couldn't imagine what that must have felt like. It was bad enough sitting through her ex's trials, with a parade of mistresses Gia had known nothing about strutting to and from the witness stand, but at least she hadn't walked in on him with any of them. And she didn't know what she'd have done if she had. "What did you do?"

"Lost my mind. I already knew what Rusty was by then, after the incident at prom, and I'd put all the other times he'd tried to best me into perspective, but the fact that Amanda would have gone along with him. Well . . . that broke my heart." He sucked in a deep, shuddering breath, giving himself a moment to calm down before continuing. "I wish I could say I'm proud of the dignified way I handled the situation, but I'd be lying to both of us. I yelled, I screamed, I jacked Rusty against the wall and threatened to kill him."

"But you didn't." She held her breath.

"No. No, I didn't." He looked her dead in the eye. "Not then or now."

She nodded. "And you didn't lay a hand on Amanda."

He shot her a dirty look. "Of course not."

"It wasn't a question, Cole. I already know you never would have done something to hurt her."

"But that's just it. I did hurt her. When I stormed out, she ran after me, begged me to listen to her, swore it wasn't what I thought, but I couldn't see past the betrayal."

"Do you think she could have been telling the truth?" Somehow, the entire situation would be that much more tragic if Cole had been mistaken.

He shrugged and plated three orders before saying anything else. "No. I know what I walked in on that day. She may have regretted it afterward, but in that moment . . . she'd been as guilty as Rusty."

She didn't push it. What would be the point? Either way, it had all ended a long time ago. "What ended up happening?"

"Rusty tracked me down at a dive we used to hang out at. He told me if I didn't leave town, leave Amanda, he'd go to the police and file charges against me — assault, attempted murder, whatever he could get to stick."

"So you left."

He nodded. "I did. Not because I was afraid of him or afraid of facing what I'd done, but because Amanda would have had to testify to the truth of what she'd seen that day. And I was ashamed of that man. So, you can see now that I practically handed her to him."

Gia bristled. "A woman is not property,

Cole. You didn't give her to him. She made her own choices."

"I guess you're right. I know you're right. But still, I walked away and never looked back. And until the other day, I never saw or heard from either of them again. I'd see mention of his business dealings on occasion, saw the announcement when they were married, and then I removed them both from all of my social media, stopped keeping tabs, and moved on with my life."

Alone. He didn't say it. He didn't have to. And not only had he been left alone, Amanda blamed him for leaving her. Which was totally bogus, because she didn't have to marry Rusty. She could have walked away, could have sought Cole out, apologized, begged him to try again, could have learned a lesson and started over with someone new. Either way, she'd made her own choice to marry that monster, for whatever her reasons.

"And now, when I finally thought I'd found happiness with Cybil, it seems Rusty's going to take that too." He sighed, shoulders sagging in defeat.

"Only if you let him, Cole."

He cracked an egg against the side of a bowl too hard, shattering the shell and dropping pieces everywhere.

Gia took it from him. "Why don't you take a minute to get yourself together, and I'll catch up here."

He nodded, yanked off his gloves and tossed them in the garbage, ripped off his apron and slammed it into the hamper, then stormed out. The sound of the back door banging shut reached her a moment later.

Maybe it was time to have another chat with Amanda. If nothing else, she could at least try to find out what she'd been doing in the forest on the morning her husband had been killed.

CHAPTER EIGHTEEN

When Cole returned, still sullen but back on the ball at the grill, Gia left him alone. For a while. Ultimately, she needed to know if he'd been the one to schedule a meeting with Rusty. He'd said he never saw Rusty or Amanda again before they came into the café, but the receipt for the muffins had been generated after the confrontation. So how did his number end up on the back of an All-Day Breakfast Café receipt? Cole would have had to contact Rusty afterward. Or Amanda. Could he have set up the appointment with her? Given her his number, and she'd jotted down the information on whatever was handy?

With the lunch rush behind them, Gia and Cole began to clean up and prep for dinner and the following morning. When Cole started washing dishes that wouldn't fit in the dishwasher and handing them to Gia to dry, she figured it was as good a time as any to approach the subject of the alleged meeting.

"Can I ask you something?"

"Sure." Cole handed her a clean stainless-steel bowl.

While she dried, she turned her back to the counter and leaned against it, facing Cole. "Do you know how your name and number got on the back of the receipt for the muffins?"

"I have no idea."

"You didn't set up any kind of meeting with him?" Or Amanda, but considering his reaction to her, she'd let that go for now.

He slammed the faucet handle down, grabbed a towel to dry his hands, and whirled to face her. "I'm telling you the truth, Gia. I have had no contact with that man or Amanda in years."

"So why were you so closed off about everything?"

He mimicked Gia's position against the island counter and folded his arms. "Because I had no idea what he might have set in motion. Rusty is mean as a rattlesnake, but slick too. And patient. He'll wait years to get revenge on someone if that's what it takes, but he always comes out on top."

"Not this time," she gently reminded him.

"No." His rigid posture relaxed, shoulders

slumped. "No, not this time."

"Question is, who would be angry enough to want him dead?"

He lifted his hands to the sides, shook his head. "I have no idea."

"Do you think Amanda could have killed him?" She held her breath, hoping she hadn't overstepped.

"Twenty years ago, I'd have said no way. The woman I knew wouldn't have had it in her to kill." He looked straight at Gia. "But I'd also have sworn that woman wouldn't cheat on me. Sometimes, we're blinded by love."

No one knew that better than Gia. And it had almost cost her everything.

"Listen." He straightened and took the dry bowl from her hand. "I'm going to start prepping for tomorrow. I'll do the western omelet mix and whatever else we're short on, and then I'll close up after dinner with Willow and Skyla. Why don't you get out of here, have Savannah drive you home?"

The thought sounded amazing, way too good to pass up. "You're sure, Cole?"

"Positive." He offered a tentative smile, no doubt to soften the blow. "You look like you're about to fall off your feet."

"All right. Let me just get Harley's dinner together, and I'll pick Thor up and go home." She put together an omelet and a sandwich, then added a big container of home fries and packed them all up in a bag with condiments and plastic utensils. Since Harley wasn't able to go inside buildings, Gia had set up a table and chairs behind the café and left dinner out for him every evening. Sometimes, he didn't show up, but most often he did. When she pushed the back door open, she found him sitting at the table.

She jumped, startled. "Oh, Harley, hey. I wasn't expecting you."

"Sorry. Didn't mean to scare you." He shook his long blonde hair, streaked with more gray than when they'd first met, out of his face and gestured toward Cole's car parked in its usual spot beside the back door. "I saw Cole's car."

"Yeah, he came in a little while ago."

"Is he okay?" Harley was a sweetheart, always worried about his friends, always looking out for those in need.

"It seems like he's as good as could be expected under the circumstances." Gia set out his dinner then sat on the chair across from him where Donna Mae sometimes joined him. "Can I ask you something?"

"Sure." He started eating.

"Did you see Cole in the forest this morning?"

With his mouth full, he nodded.

Experience had taught her Harley would answer most of her questions, but he didn't ever offer information. Giving him a moment to enjoy his dinner, she tried to figure out how to best phrase what she wanted to know to get answers without having to ask a million questions. "Did you see Rusty?"

"Yeah."

"Before he was killed?"

He shook his head.

Pulling information out of Harley was like wringing blood from a stone. Not that he didn't want to be helpful, he just wasn't the most social creature. "When I saw you by the river, it looked like you were washing your hands. Was something wrong?"

He scrunched up his face. "Poison ivy. Got it all over me."

"On your hands?"

"And my arms."

"How'd you manage that?"

Not that she was that knowledgeable about poison ivy, though she should be if she wanted to continue to walk in the woods, but it seemed more likely you'd brush up against it with your feet or legs.

"Donna Mae dropped her phone in the

brush, so I dug around and picked it up before I noticed."

That made sense. "Is that when you saw Cole?"

"No. That's when the lady screamed."

Whoa. That was new. "What lady, Harley? Did Cybil scream when they found Rusty? Did you see another woman in the forest?"

Unfazed by the rush of adrenaline that prompted the barrage of questions, Harley stared at her, blinking repeatedly.

She clamped her teeth together to stem the torrent, took a calming breath. "Sorry. Too many at once."

He nodded, continuing to eat his sandwich.

"Okay. Do you know who screamed?"

He shook his head. "Could have been the lady with the hat."

The video footage Alfie had found showed both Amanda and Ariyah entering the forest that morning. Could one of them have screamed? "Can you describe what the woman looked like?"

"She had a hat."

Gia counted to ten in her head. "Did you notice anything else?"

"It was one of those ones with the big brim. I couldn't see her face."

"Okay." She nodded. She'd have to try to

talk to Donna Mae, ask her if she'd seen anyone, though if she had, she probably would have already told the police when they'd questioned her.

Harley frowned, tilted his head to the side. "Or I guess it could have been the policeman. It sounded like a woman, though."

"What policeman? Officer Erickson?"

He nodded thoughtfully as he chewed.

"But he didn't come until after Cole and Cybil found Rusty, right?"

"Maybe. I don't remember."

"Okay. Don't worry about it." But she'd pass the information on to Hunt, see if maybe he could find anyone else who'd witnessed the woman in the hat. "Thank you, Harley."

"Sure." He continued to eat.

Figuring she'd pressured him enough, Gia let it go and just sat with him, enjoying his company while he ate. "Where's Donna Mae tonight?"

"Still working." His eyes lit with pleasure. "She's meeting me at the park later."

"I'm so happy you two found each other again and have become such good friends."

"Me too." He finished off his potatoes, then put the garbage back into the bag and crumpled it up. "Thank you for dinner."

"Of course. Did you eat enough?"

He patted his belly and nodded.

Gia was glad to see he'd filled out a little since the day she'd first found him hanging over the side of her dumpster. "If you can hang around for a few minutes, I'll grab some scones for you to take to the park and share with Donna Mae later."

He grinned. "I'd like that. Thanks."

Gia took the garbage from him and hurried inside to get his dessert before he could wander off. After giving Harley his bag of scones, Gia told him to say hi to Donna Mae for her, then hurried back inside. A quick glance at the clock over the cutout assured her she'd have enough time for a quick trip to Orlando before Zoe would close the doggie daycare for the night. She could call Hunt on the way and tell him what Harley had seen.

She found Savannah behind the counter making a cold brew. "Hey. You up for a quick ride to Orlando to see if we can find Rhonda?"

"You betcha." She capped the to-go cup and turned to the register. "I'll meet you out front as soon as I finish with my last two tables."

Since both tables appeared to be finishing up, Gia collected her bag from the office, said goodbye to Skyla and Willow then stepped out front to call Zoe. Puffy white clouds stacked high into the brilliant blue sky, hovering gently, offering sporadic bits of relief from the otherwise relentless sunshine.

It took four rings for Zoe to pick up, sounding winded. "Hey, Gia. What's up?"

Gia nodded and smiled at a customer entering the café, then shifted to stand by the apartment door so she wouldn't block the entrance. "I wanted to take a quick run to Orlando before I pick up Thor, if that's okay?"

"Of course. If you don't make it back in time, you know I don't mind taking him with me when I leave. You can either swing by and pick him up at Trevor's later, or I'll bring him back here with me in the morning."

A smile tugged at her. She was so happy to see Trevor and Zoe hitting it off so well. When she'd first met Trevor, he'd awkwardly but adorably asked her out, but it didn't take long for both of them to realize they were better as friends — good friends. "Thanks. I appreciate it, but I should make it back in time. And if not, it's really comforting to know he'll be taken care of."

"If by taken care of you mean spoiled rotten in that mansion of his, you're not kidding."

Gia laughed as she disconnected. Trevor was the only person she'd ever heard of with a potty pavilion for his dogs, complete with grooming area and doggie playground that he decorated for Christmas. Spoiled was an understatement.

With a few minutes to spare after leaving a message for Hunt, Gia strolled down Main Street. When she saw Trevor outside Storm Scoopers serving a family of four at a wrought iron table, she waved. Since he waved back without running over to talk to her, she figured he was busy. Actually . . . She looked up and down Main Street, lined with parked cars. Seemed everyone was busier than usual. Most likely, people were scared knowing a killer was on the loose and looking for information. And what better place to find it than the Boggy Creek rumor mill — a.k.a. Main Street?

A quick peek into what would have been Rusty's shop netted nothing new. Still empty. Still locked. Then Savannah emerged, halting any further investigation. Probably for the best. There didn't seem to be anything to see in the shop anyway. As she strode to Savannah's car, she couldn't help wondering what kind of shop would open now that the deli was off the table.

She slid into the passenger seat as Savannah opened her blue Mustang's convertible top. "Thanks for taking a ride with me. I don't really feel up to going all the way home before heading to Orlando."

"Don't worry about it. I'm just as eager to get to the bottom of all this as you are." She winked and slid her sunglasses on, covering the stress in her eyes. "So, did you hear the latest?"

"That depends on what the latest is."

With a quick glance to be sure no one was coming, Savannah pulled out onto Main Street and headed toward the highway. "Caleb Ryan was picked up for questioning."

"Oh, yeah? Did you talk to Leo?"

"Nah. He's been incommunicado all day, so all I have is gossip." She grinned at Gia. "But since it came from the Bailey twins, I'm pretty sure it's probably accurate."

"No kidding." How the two elderly women managed to find out so much and have most of it be true was beyond Gia. "Did they know why he was brought in?"

Savannah shrugged. "The details are a little sketchy, but supposedly the police have reason to believe Caleb was in the area where Rusty's body was found."

A smile tugged at her. Of course, Hunt

would have found the security camera footage Trevor had unearthed. "Along with Ariyah and Amanda."

"Wait. What?" Savannah eased on the brakes and glanced at her. "You talked to Hunt?"

"No. I haven't heard from him."

She shot Gia a friendly scowl. "You didn't leave the back all day. How did you hear that?"

She laughed. Since they'd been too busy all day for her to update Savannah, she ran through the surveillance video footage Alfie had been able to pull up, then told her about the conversation with Cole, minus the derailed proposal he'd asked her to keep quiet about. It didn't sit well keeping anything from Savannah, but her friend would understand that wasn't Gia's secret to tell. "Anyway, if Caleb was picked up for questioning, that blows our woman scorned theory."

"Not necessarily," Savannah argued. "You said Amanda was there too. Maybe Caleb's not a suspect but a witness."

CHAPTER NINETEEN

Savannah turned onto a narrow two-lane street in Orlando, about as far from the beaches, orange groves, and theme parks on the postcards filling souvenir shops as you could get. Boarded, graffiti-covered strip malls dotted the area. Women clad in spandex and vacant expressions sauntered down the cracked sidewalks. Men and women huddled in alleys, casting suspicious gazes over their shoulders every now and then before quickly making an exchange.

One man in particular caught Gia's attention as he strolled down the street, bottle-shaped brown paper bag swinging from one hand. He was dressed in dirty, torn jeans and a bold Hawaiian-print shirt. His hair hung in skimpy strands over his shoulders and down his back. But it was the broad smile on his face that drew the eye. No matter what life had dealt him, the man seemed happy.

"Is this the turn?" Savannah asked, pulling Gia's attention from the man.

Gia checked the GPS on her phone. "No. You make the next right after the light."

She nodded and stepped on her brakes, stopping for the red light. A man clad in cut-off sweat shorts and a white tank top, dreadlocks spilling down his back, earbuds plugged into his ears, bopped into the intersection to a tune only he could hear.

Savannah grinned as he executed a few hip-hop-style moves, spun, and bowed, then danced onto the next corner. "I love coming to Orlando."

"How could you not?" This was a part of town Gia had never visited before, a run-down area known for its crime, streetwalkers, and drug dealers, and yet it had such an energetic vibe. "Here."

Savannah made the turn onto a cobblestone roadway. Brick buildings, squat houses, and garbage-strewn empty lots lined the way.

Gia checked the address. "It's that apartment building right there."

The two-story faded brick building looked like it might once have been a hotel. Doors stood open, laundry hung from lines crisscrossing every which way, and kids watched the car with suspicion in their too-old eyes before darting away. A woman's screams had Gia holding her breath for a moment, then a teenager shot from an open doorway followed by a slipper bouncing off his back and an irate woman in a housedress yelling after him as he laughed and danced out of the way.

Savannah rolled slowly through the lot, then tapped the brakes as a skinny grayish brown dog darted in front of them. She watched the animal disappear between buildings. "You know, a lot of Native American tribes consider them to be a good omen."

"Dogs?"

Savannah laughed and shook her head. "It wasn't a dog, Gia. It's a coyote."

No wonder the kids had all bolted. She'd thought they were running from a strange vehicle.

She started forward again, rolling through the lot lest anything else dart into her path. "According to legend, they're often seen as helpful spirit animals that can guide you on a journey."

Gia stared after the animal, but it didn't reappear. "Let's hope this one guided us to a place where we can get some answers."

She held up her crossed fingers. "Here's hoping."

"It's the end unit over there, second floor." Gia pointed toward the back of the lot.

Savannah got as close as she could and parked, then raised the top, climbed out, and locked the doors.

They passed the teen who'd been tossed or fled his apartment sulking against the far wall and jogged up the stairs to apartment 10B. Since both the front and back doors stood open, Gia could see straight through the apartment to an abandoned gas station surrounded by a chain-link fence that had seen better days. She knocked on the doorjamb. "Hello?"

A woman emerged from the kitchen area at the back of the apartment. "What da y'all want? In case y'all cayn't tell, I ain't got no money, so if yer sellin' somethin', you can just skedaddle."

"I'm sorry to bother you." Gia spared Savannah a quick glance. She already knew she'd found her quarry, recognized the once-attractive woman from her MySpace profile photo, though the years had not been kind. Age or stress or a combination of the two had left Rhonda beat up and dejected. Deep lines creased her face, jowls sagged, and more salt than pepper streaked her limp hair. "I'm looking for Rhonda Kirkman."

"Well, you found her." The woman narrowed her gaze. "Whadda y'all want?"

"My name is Gia Morelli, and this is my friend Savannah." Since the woman didn't invite them in, Gia leaned a shoulder against the doorjamb. "I'm hoping you can give me some information on Rusty Bragge."

"If you're lookin' to hear anything kind about that man, you oughtta just keep right on walkin'." She started to turn away.

"Actually, Mrs. Kirkman, Rusty was murdered the other morning, and we're trying to figure out who killed him."

That stopped her in her tracks, and she turned back toward them. "If you figure it out, lemme know. I wanna be the first to shake his hand."

As far as openings went, it was probably the best she could hope for. "I take it you didn't care for him then?"

She scoffed and folded her arms across her chest.

"Do you mind if I ask why you were friends with him on social media?"

"Social media? What are you talkin' about?" She gestured toward the apartment's interior, where Gia could see a battered couch, an ancient television, and a table with two chairs, one of the legs duct taped. "Does it look like I can afford a computer to you?"

"I'm sorry, ma'am. This was an old My-Space account we came across."

"MySpace?" Her thick brows dove together over empty green eyes that had sparkled in a picture taken a lifetime ago. "Oh, right. That was me and Jim's account. Long time ago, that was."

Gia almost turned away and left this woman to her misery, and would have if not for Cole. She owed it to him to get whatever answers she could. "Mrs. Kirkman, a friend of mine is being questioned in his murder, and I am trying to prove his innocence. If there's anything you can tell me about Rusty Bragge or what happened between him and your husband, anything at all, I'm hoping it might help."

"What's your friend's name?"

"Cole. Cole Barrister."

Recognition sparked in her eyes. "He was Jim's friend once. And then he wasn't."

"I'm so sorry."

She spent another moment sizing up Gia and then Savannah, and finally stepped back for them to enter. "May as well come on in if we're gonna get into all of that."

Hope soared. She had no idea if it would prove helpful, but at least it seemed she might find out something. When Rhonda grabbed a straight-backed chair from the table, turned it to face the couch, and sat, Gia perched on the edge of the couch facing her.

Savannah sat beside Gia. "Thank you so much for speaking to us, Mrs. Kirkman."

She waved it off. "May as well call me Rhonda."

"Thank you, Rhonda," Gia said sincerely. "What can you tell us about Rusty and Jim's relationship?"

"Relationship? Hah. There was nothin' between those two but animosity, and that was all on Rusty. My Jim . . ." Tears shimmered in her eyes, and Gia didn't have the heart to ask what had happened between them. Hopefully, Rhonda would see fit to tell the story. But one look around the shabby apartment was all it took to see the woman now lived alone. "Jim was a good man, too good, if I'm bein' honest. He never could see the bad in people, and that horrible man took such advantage of him. It was painful to watch."

Gia reached for Rhonda's hand, gripped it in hers for a moment, and squeezed. "I'm so sorry, Rhonda."

She only nodded, gripped Gia's hand like a lifeline for a moment, then released her and wiped the tears that had tipped over and tracked down her cheeks. "I guess I should back up a bit first. When Jim and Rusty were still in high school, that monster framed him, made Cole think Jim was the one who put drugs in his locker and got him in trouble. Even though those two were thick as thieves back then, Cole should have questioned why Jim would do something like that."

Gia cringed at the censure in her tone. "Cole told me what happened back then, and I know it's probably no consolation, but he shoulders a tremendous amount of guilt over what happened."

She offered a noncommittal shrug. "Guess that saves me the trouble of rehashin' then. Did he tell you about when Rusty tried to kill Jim?"

"What?" She sat up straighter. Could that be the attempted murder charge no one seemed to be able to find out much about? "No, he didn't."

"Well, I cayn't say fer sure Cole knew about it. He'd already cut Jim out of his life before it all went down. But after that whole mess, Jim wanted to make it right with Cole, told a friend he was gonna talk to him, explain how it wasn't him that did it and that it must have been Rusty because he was the only other person with the combination to Cole's locker. That friend betrayed him, ratted him out to Rusty."

She sniffed and wiped her cheeks with both hands. "Rusty went after Jim, ambushed him, beat him within an inch of his life, put him in the hospital."

That made sense of the charge, but why reduce it? "And they charged him with attempted murder?"

"Yeah, for like a minute."

"What do you mean?"

"Thanks to Rusty's pack of witnesses all shakin' in their boots and swearin' Jim started the fight, which he absolutely did not, and a well-connected daddy with a judge in his pocket, the charges got bumped down, he did community service, and his record was sealed."

"So how did you end up friends with him on MySpace?"

"A couple a years later, after Jim started a successful air-conditionin' business, Rusty showed up in town. Said he wanted to make amends and all that. He was nothing but a lyin' snake, but Jim couldn't see it. He was too kind to see that some people are just plain bad. Evil, if you know what I mean."

Gia nodded. "I do, yes."

"So, anyway, they got to bein' friends again, then Jim started takin' him on calls, teaching him the business. And Rusty stole his customers right out from under him, opened a business in the same area. Which would have been okay. Not like there's a shortage of air conditioners that need fixin' in Florida. But Rusty wrote up a bunch of bad reviews, trashed Jim's reputation, and, I can't prove this, mind you, but a couple a Jim's jobs went bad, one unit even shorted out and started a fire, and I'd bet anything Rusty had gone back and sabotaged those units. He left Jim devastated. Jim blamed himself, first for thinkin' he made a mistake installing the unit, then for believing in Rusty." She paused, took a deep, shaky breath, blew her nose. "Anyway, everything went down hill after that. We wound up livin' here, and Jim lost all confidence in himself. There weren't no fight left in 'im. Then one day, he just up and left. Never came back. Been a lot of years gone by since then."

"Oh, Rhonda, I'm so sorry." Gia swallowed down the lump clogging her throat, desperately wishing she had something more to offer this woman than her sympathy. "I can't understand how that man could have gotten away with ruining so many lives."

"Because he's a predator," Savannah said

softly. "And he knew the kind of people he could prey on — people who were kind, sensitive."

Rhonda nodded through tears. "Just like my Jim."

Savannah's expression hardened, and for a moment, Gia regretted bringing her, opening up old wounds. "Well, you don't have to worry about him hurting anyone else, Rhonda."

Her lips quivered into a tentative smile. "I won't go so far as to say I'm happy he's dead — the Lord don't take kindly to reveling in another's misfortune — but I will say I'm glad he won't be able to do no more harm."

Gia couldn't bring herself to ask the question begging for an answer. From everything Rhonda had already said, she doubted Jim would have killed Rusty. It seemed when it came to fighting back, Jim most often chose to flee.

"Can I ask you somethin' now?" Rhonda's eyes were puffy, but the tears had finally subsided.

"Sure." And she prayed she'd have an answer.

"Are you gonna try to talk to Jim now?"

"I am if I can find him." Though him being homeless would certainly make it more difficult. There was no guarantee he'd even stayed in Florida.

"Oh, you don't have to find him. I know right where he is."

"You do?"

"Of course I do. Just 'cause he left don't mean I don't keep track of my man." She stood and grabbed a piece of paper off the table, turned it over, and jotted something down on the back.

Figuring she was done talking, and sorry to have dragged up such painful memories, Gia stood to leave.

"Do me a favor?" Rhonda pressed the paper with directions written on it into Gia's hand. "When you find Jim and tell him Rusty's dead, tell him I'm still waitin' on him to come home."

Gia's hand shook as she held on to Rhonda's hand for a moment. "I'll tell him. Thank you."

She only nodded and turned away.

Not knowing what else she could say to ease this woman's pain, Gia walked out.

Savannah lowered her gaze and fell into step beside her, waiting until they were out of earshot of the apartment to speak. "Do you think Jim could have killed him?"

"I'd say no, but I don't know. There's no telling what someone might do when he's broken."

"I can't believe how many lives that man ruined." Savannah stomped down the metal staircase.

"Yeah, well, we can't do anything about the past, but I can promise you one thing. Rusty won't be adding Cole to his list."

CHAPTER TWENTY

Savannah followed the directions Gia read from the page Rhonda had given her through a downtrodden neighborhood near the stadium. Though they located the small tent encampment Rhonda insisted Jim lived in, they found no sign of him. "What do you want to do now?"

Giving up, Gia lay her head back against the seat and closed her eyes. Maybe Alfie could figure out a way to find him. "Go home and sleep for about twelve hours."

Savannah laughed. "Girl, you couldn't sleep twelve hours if you tried."

"True enough, but five or six sure would be nice." She stretched, easing the ache in her back.

With nowhere left to look, Savannah turned toward the turnpike. "Are you going to let Zoe take Thor home, or do you want to swing by and pick him up?"

Gia checked the dashboard clock. Going

back into town would add at least twenty minutes to her trip, but she'd barely spent any time with Thor in the past two days, and she missed him terribly. "If you don't mind running by the café, I think we can make it before Zoe leaves for the night."

"Sure."

"If you don't feel up to it, you can drop me off home, and I'll pick him up at Trevor's."

"Oh, yeah?" Savannah waggled her eyebrows. "Those two are getting pretty tight, huh?"

"It seems like it. I'm so happy. Trevor's such a nice guy, it's great to see him with someone who appreciates him so much."

Savannah frowned.

"What? You don't agree?"

"About Zoe and Trevor? No . . . I mean yes . . . I agree Zoe and Trevor make a great couple. I was just thinking about Rhonda and Jim. It was heartbreaking to see how much she still cares for him."

The thought brought an ache to her chest. "I know. I wish we could have found him and brought him home to her."

"Yeah, me too."

Gia stared out the window, watching the palm trees and fields pass by, enjoying the herds of cows lazily grazing. "Rhonda said he spends all his time in the encampment. You don't think the fact that he wasn't there means he did it, do you?"

Savannah was already shaking her head. "We're strangers, Gia. And after the betrayal he suffered at the hands of what he thought of as a good friend, it's no surprise he'd lay low if he found out we were looking for him."

"You're probably right." She hoped.

Savannah quirked a brow. "Just probably?"

"Fine." Gia grinned. "Usually."

"That's better." She flipped the radio to a country station and let it play quietly in the background. "Anyway, I'll go to the café with you and pick up Thor from daycare."

"You're sure?"

"Yup. Leo won't be home anyway, not when he's smack in the middle of a homicide investigation." She checked her rearview mirror, switched lanes. Not the best time of day to navigate the area, between tourists searching for restaurants and residents trying to get home from work.

"No. Hunt probably won't stop by either, unless they drop in together for something to eat." Not that she had anything in the house to feed them other than leftover appetizers. "You want to grab a few pizzas on the way home? Maybe see if Alfie wants to come over for a bit? Then you can see the security videos yourself."

Savannah nodded. "If Cole's still at work, you could ask him and Cybil over too."

"We'll see if he left yet. I don't want to interrupt if he's with Cybil." Maybe he'd work up the courage to open up and let her in, or at the very least admit he'd messed up and try to repair their relationship.

"How is he doing? Really?"

"He seemed okay. Tired more than anything." And stubborn.

"Okay, well, pizza it is then." She hit her blinker and moved over to exit the turnpike, humming absently along with the radio. "You know, I was thinking."

A song about love and cheating and broken hearts played in the background. Maybe she ought to change the station. "About?"

"Maybe it's time to pay Amanda another visit, just ask her what she was doing in the forest that morning."

"Don't you think we should leave that to Hunt and Leo?"

Her brows shot all the way up beneath her bangs. "Since when?"

"Okay, okay." Gia couldn't help but laugh at the horror in her expression. "I'll tell you what. We'll go home, eat some pizza, and make up a suspect list so we know exactly what we're dealing with. I'll text Hunt and Leo now and let them know the plan in case they can get a few minutes free to stop and eat."

Savannah nodded and turned toward the café.

"Then, if we still think it's warranted, I'll swing by Amanda's hotel on the way to work tomorrow and see if she's feeling any chattier than she was the other day." Though Gia didn't like her as the killer. She couldn't explain why. Maybe it was just wishful thinking, knowing how badly it would hurt Cole if it turned out she'd murdered Rusty. Even though he had nothing to do with the crime, hadn't even seen Amanda in years, Gia knew him well enough to know he'd shoulder some amount of guilt anyway.

They remained quiet the rest of the trip, but for the music, which had thankfully perked up, each of them lost in their own thoughts, no doubt both running to murder. Savannah parked in front of the café. "The lights are still on, so I guess Cole's still here."

Gia fished her key out of her bag, then got out and ran to the door. Thunder rumbled in the distance, where dark clouds had begun to gather and build. Lightning forked toward the ground. She opened the door and hurried inside. Hopefully, she could talk to Cole quickly and run down to Zoe's before those clouds opened up. While Savannah stopped to restock the dining room, she found Cole in back cleaning the grill. "Hey, Cole. What's going on?"

He paused and glanced her way. "Hey. What are you doing back? I thought you were going home to sleep?"

"Yeah, well, so did I, but something came up."

"Oh?" He returned to scrubbing with a wire brush. "And what was so important?"

She found she was suddenly nervous. What if Cole was angry she'd pursued Rhonda? What if he didn't want her knowing all about his past? There was only one way to find out. So, she did what any mature woman would do in her situation. "Willow and Skyla left already?"

He studied her for a moment, then accepted the change of subject. "Yup. They were going to a play at the community center. Willow said she'd be in early to restock the dining room."

"I'll text her not to worry about it." She pulled out her phone, scrolled for Willow's number. "Savannah's doing it now."

Cole finished with the grill, washed his

hands, and dried them on a towel he then tossed into the hamper along with his apron. When he turned, humor lit his eyes. "So, now that we did that dance, want to tell me what's really going on?"

She sighed. She should have known she wouldn't get away with avoiding him. "I went to see Rhonda Kirkman."

"Rhonda?" He scowled. "Why would you do that?"

"I wanted to talk to Jim."

He schooled his expression but couldn't dim the hope that flared in his eyes. "Was he there?"

She hated to dampen that small spark. "He wasn't. I'm sorry."

He nodded, avoiding her gaze.

She told him what Rhonda had shared, blurting it all out in one big rush, like ripping off a Band-Aid, and ended with, "I'm sorry we couldn't find him, but we're going to look again."

He was quiet for a moment, contemplating everything she'd said. "No."

"You don't want me to look for him?" It seemed cruel to just leave him out there without trying to help in some way, even if just to let him know Rusty couldn't hurt him anymore.

"If you don't mind, I'll do it." He held

out his hand, and Gia handed him the paper Rhonda had given her. He studied it for a moment before stuffing it into the pocket of his khakis. "It's long past time I apologized to him. Who knows? Maybe I can do something to help him get his life back on track. I owe him that much, at least."

"Okay, but if there's anything I can do, just let me know."

"Sure, thanks." He wrapped his arms around her, pulled her close. "For everything, Gia. Thank you for standing by me, for believing in me."

"Hey." She rubbed circles on his back. "How many times were you there for me when I needed help? Did you expect anything less?"

He pulled back, grinned through tears shimmering in his bottom lashes. "Nope. I knew you'd have my back, and Savannah too, but knowing it doesn't make me appreciate it any less."

"We'll always be there for you, Cole." She scanned the kitchen, in perfect order to open the following morning. No surprise. "Speaking of helping, Savannah and I are going to grab some pizzas then head out to my house to try to organize some of the information we've gathered over the past couple of days. If you and Cybil want to join us, we'd be happy to have you."

He was already nodding. "Absolutely. I'll pick Cybil up and meet you out there."

"Great. Who knows? Maybe you can make sense of something everyone else is missing, since you're familiar with at least some of the players and past events we may not even realize are relevant." Thunder boomed, loud enough to make Gia jump. "I'd better get Thor before it starts pouring."

"Just lock the front door behind you, and I'll lock up the back on my way out." He pulled his keys out of his pocket. "And I'll pick up the pizzas on my way over."

She started to protest, but he cut her off.

"It'll be easier that way. You can get Thor home and settled before I get there with the food, then we can dive right into the investigation."

"All right, thank you." She would have refused, insisted she'd invited him and he didn't have to do that, but for the first time since seeing Rusty — or probably Amanda — in the café, he seemed himself, ready to tackle the situation head-on. So, instead, she thanked him again and jogged through the dining room, calling to Savannah on the way out, "I'm going to run down and get Thor before it rains."

"I'm just gonna finish up here, and I'll

pick you up out in front of Zoe's."

Main Street wasn't half as crowded as it had been earlier. The sidewalks had cleared, probably in deference to the coming storm. She breathed in deeply, enjoying the scent of ozone preceding the rain. Black clouds roiled overhead, the rumble of thunder almost constant. Lightning sizzled between the clouds. But the wind had yet to pick up, so she held on to hope she'd make it to Zoe's before the storm unleashed its full fury.

The first fat raindrops plopped down as she was passing the old hardware store. Light spilled out onto the sidewalk, and as she moved closer, she noticed movement inside. A man and a woman stood facing each other in front of a counter.

The woman waved her arms while speaking rapidly. The man Gia recognized as Caleb Ryan stood with his feet apart, arms crossed over his chest. What would Caleb be doing in Rusty's shop? Obviously, the deal would fall through now that Rusty had passed away, but there's no way the legalities of it all could have been straightened out yet. The police hadn't even released his body.

She stopped beside the brick wall, hoping not to be seen, and peered into the window.

If Gia had to guess from the brief moment she witnessed of the interaction, she'd say they were arguing.

She looked up at the threatening sky and had only a moment to make a choice — continue on to the doggy daycare two doors down, or stop in and see if she could get any information. If nothing else, maybe she could find out who the woman was. She shot Savannah a quick text, asking her to pick her up in front of the old hardware store, then tucked her phone into her bag, took a deep breath, and pulled the door open.

CHAPTER TWENTY-ONE

"Can I help you?" Caleb turned on Gia the instant she stepped inside, his stance no less combative than he'd appeared with the woman.

When no spark of recognition flared, Gia figured it was a safe bet he didn't recognize her from their brief passing in the hotel hallway and let the door fall closed behind her just as a tropical downpour let loose. "I'm sorry to intrude. I was walking from the café to the doggy daycare when the storm started. I saw the lights on in here, and my friend is picking me up in a minute or two, but I thought maybe I could just hang out here by the door until she pulls up?"

Caleb studied her, then turned her attention to the woman Gia now recognized from her picture on the computer.

Brynleigh Colton, the inexplicably wealthy treasurer of the zoning commission who they suspected was taking bribes. Of course, it was always possible she had family money. They hadn't had a chance to delve that far into her yet. She made a mental note to check that once she got home. "Does that mean it's okay if I wait?"

"Yeah, whatever." Caleb waved a hand in dismissal, then propped his hands on his hips and stared daggers at Brynleigh.

Oo-kay. Now what? He clearly wasn't going to engage in any kind of small talk with Gia, nor was he going to return to his argument with Brynleigh. Too bad. Gia would have loved to know the source of their tension. Maybe she could still learn something. She plastered on a smile and stepped toward him, hand extended. "I'm Gia Morelli, by the way."

"Look, I —" That was as far as he got before recognition slammed through him. His eyes widened for a fraction of a second before narrowing in suspicion. "What are you doing here?"

"I . . . uh . . ." She hooked a thumb over her shoulder. "I already told you, I was leaving work and going to pick my dog up from daycare when it started pouring. Rather than get in my friend's car soaked to the bone, I thought maybe I could wait inside."

Okay, stop rambling now, Gia. A terrible

habit, rambling when caught doing something she probably shouldn't have been. And she was going to stop, right now. Even if only out loud.

Anger flamed, brightening his dull yellow eyes. "You were at the hotel the other day. I saw you when I was leaving —"

"I'm Brynleigh Colton." Brynleigh stepped in front of him and held a hand out to Gia. "It's a pleasure to meet you."

Shifting her gaze from Caleb to Brynleigh, Gia shook her hand. "It's nice to meet you too."

Though her pulse pounded painfully hard, Gia ignored it. If only ignoring Caleb's presence was as easy, she might be able to learn something from Brynleigh, though it wasn't likely the woman would blurt out that she was corrupt, or a killer, or even an accessory. Maybe she and Caleb had conspired to kill Rusty?

When the silence stretched to the point of awkwardness, Gia gestured around the shop, feigning interest in an attempt to put some distance between her and the unusually large man. She had a split second to decide how much to admit knowing. Would they buy she hadn't heard Rusty was opening a deli? Probably not. "So, are you planning on opening a shop here?"

Caleb opened his mouth to say something, probably nothing nice if his expression was any indication.

Brynleigh moved to intercept again, her smile more of a predatory leer. "Mr. Ryan is considering taking over the store from Mr. Bragge's estate."

Keeping an eye on Caleb in her peripheral vision, Gia fell into step with Brynleigh as she not so discreetly ushered her toward the front door. Rain beat furiously against the display windows, washing down them in a torrent, making it almost impossible to see outside. "What kind of shop is he planning to open?"

"A bakery."

Huh. That actually sounded like a good idea, *if* she was telling the truth, considering Hunt had said he'd wanted to open an office. But a bakery would only add to the appeal of Main Street without competing with any of the existing establishments. She'd be lying to herself if she didn't admit to a wave of relief. Although, the brooding man standing next to her didn't appear to have the personality for a mom-and-pop-style business. But, to be fair, she'd only seen him at his worst. Maybe he was a nice guy who was just wrapped up in the middle of something too overwhelming to deal with

— kind of like Cole. A pang of sympathy tried to surface.

If they were right about Rusty bribing Brynleigh to steal the shop out from under Caleb, she could understand his anger. Then again, was he angry enough to kill Rusty over it?

Brynleigh stopped when they reached the entryway. "I'm sorry I don't have more time to chat, but I'm in kind of a hurry, and I'm parked out back."

A shiver raced up her spine at the thought of being left alone in the shop with Caleb. "No problem. I understand completely. If you're ever in the neighborhood and have time, stop into the café and say hello."

"I sure will." She shook Gia's hand again. "It was nice to meet you, Gia. Feel free to wait here until your friend arrives."

"Thank you." She turned to Caleb. "And good luck with the bakery. I hope it works out."

He dipped his chin in acknowledgment, then turned and walked into the back room with Brynleigh.

Gia's gaze fell on the counter where the two had been standing, at a stack of papers strewn there. If she could just get one little peek. She listened intently for any sound to indicate Caleb's return. Nothing. Then again, it would be difficult to hear anything over the splattering of the rain against the windows. Maybe he and Brynleigh had disappeared to continue their argument.

A quick check out the window showed headlights, most likely Savannah sitting and waiting for her. Her friend's presence emboldened her. Surely, if Gia didn't come out in a reasonable amount of time, Savannah would come in looking for her.

Okay, it's now or never. Cook or get out of the kitchen.

Yanking her phone out of her bag as she went, she tiptoed across the room. A thick contract lay on the counter, some of the pages scattered. Already signed by Caleb, purchasing the store. Breath coming in harsh gasps she prayed Caleb wouldn't hear, she snapped pictures of each of the pages, then hightailed it back toward the door.

"You know what I find interesting?"

Her heart lurched into her throat at the sound of Caleb's harsh voice.

Had he seen her snooping? He probably hadn't noticed her taking pictures, since she'd had one eye plastered on the doorway to the back room until she was done, but he might have seen her after she'd turned and started moving away. Probably best to just shut up and see where he was going with that question.

He took a menacing step toward her. "I find it fascinating that you knew I was the one opening a business and not Brynleigh. Want to explain that?"

"I . . . uh . . ." *Think, think, think* . . . She ran back through their interaction, belatedly realizing her mistake. Instead of asking Brynleigh, who she'd been speaking to at the time, she'd turned to Caleb to ask what kind of shop he planned to open. Stupid. What could prove to be a very costly mistake.

The front door opened just then, ushering in a wave of windblown rain. Savannah poked her head in and quickly surveyed Caleb's rigid posture and couldn't miss the deer-in-the-headlights expression Gia must be wearing. "Hey, Gia. You ready to go?"

"Um, yeah." She muttered a quick "Good meeting you" to Caleb then grabbed the door from Savannah, ducked her head against the rain, and jetted out to the car. Rainwater splashed from the river running down the sidewalk, soaking her all the way to her thighs. Cold rivulets ran down the back of her neck, icing the chill that had already settled there. She ripped the passenger-side door open and practically dove inside, then slammed the door shut behind her, leaned her head back against the seat, and closed her eyes.

Savannah slammed her door and shook the rain from her hair. "Should I even ask what that was all about?"

"Probably not." She blew out a slow, calming breath. "I still have to stop for Thor."

"Don't worry about it. Trevor stopped by when I was on my way out, and he and Zoe are going to bring Thor home and stay for pizza." She checked for oncoming traffic, then pulled out slowly into the storm.

"Great, thanks." Gia turned her head without lifting it from the headrest and found Caleb standing in the open doorway staring out at her. Angry — for sure. Intimidating — absolutely. Guilty of murder — maybe. Then again, maybe he was just ticked off that she'd intruded on his privacy. Either way, she was pretty sure she'd made an enemy of her new neighbor.

Resigned to the fact there was nothing she could do to change the situation, especially not without first figuring out if Caleb was Rusty's killer, Gia sighed and sat up straighter. After giving Savannah a quick recap of what had transpired in the shop, including Caleb's attitude, she opened the camera on her phone and clicked on the pictures, then scrolled through. "I found a contract on the counter in there."

Savannah waited, the steady beat of the windshield wipers exceptionally loud in the silent confines of the small car.

"Wait a minute. That can't be right." Gia scrolled through the pictures again, enlarging one section at a time to read as Savannah drove. There was a copy of the permit for the bakery, so Brynleigh had been telling the truth about that. But it was the next page that had her heart rate kicking into overdrive. "I snapped a few quick pictures of papers that were sitting on the counter. Granted, some of them are a little blurry because I was in a hurry and watching for Caleb to return while I was taking them, but there's no mistaking the date on this page."

Savannah chanced a quick peek at the phone Gia held out, but snapped her attention right back to the road. "I can't make it out. What's wrong?"

"The contract was signed on the day Rusty was killed, and the business license for the bakery was issued the day after." No way could that have happened that quickly. It had to have been in the works beforehand. Didn't it?

Savannah shrugged. "Assuming Amanda,

269

as his spouse, would inherit all of whatever estate Rusty might have left behind, she probably just wanted to dump it all. It seems reasonable she'd sell it to Caleb, especially if my suspicion that they were having an affair is accurate."

She tried to organize a timeline in her head. She really needed to write it down, see it laid out. "Okay, assuming for a minute that's true, when would the zoning approval come through?"

Since Savannah had once been a real estate agent, she would know better than Gia. "The zoning would have to be approved before he could attain . . ."

"Exactly." Gia squinted at the date line to be absolutely sure there was no mistake. "I find it really interesting that the zoning approval came through, signed by Brynleigh Colton, two days before Rusty was killed."

CHAPTER TWENTY-TWO

When Savannah pulled into Gia's driveway, Cole and Cybil were just pulling up. She and Gia met them on the front lawn.

At least the rain had stopped. Gia hugged Cybil, so happy to see her and Cole had at least decided to stay together. "Hey, guys."

Cybil turned and hugged Savannah.

Cole just nodded, since he was cradling a stack of pizza boxes high enough to feed a small army, which Gia supposed is what they'd invited.

When Trevor pulled to the curb behind Cole, Gia handed Savannah her key to the house. "Better get Cole inside before Thor decides to greet him and we all end up sharing the stale Cheerios in my pantry for dinner."

While Savannah let Cole and Cybil in, Gia waited on the lawn.

With three dogs of his own, Trevor knew enough to wait until the front door closed before opening the back door to let Thor out.

Brandy, Trevor's German shepherd, bounded out behind him.

"Hope it's okay," Trevor called. "We didn't go home after I picked up Zoe and the boys."

"You know Brandy's always welcome here," Gia yelled back.

Thor reached her first, skidding to a stop and wagging his entire body.

Gia laughed and hugged him. "I missed you too, buddy."

Brandy stopped beside him, then turned his attention to the garage, looked up, and barked.

Thor froze mid-wag, followed Brandy's gaze up a large tree beside the garage, and started barking. He turned in a circle, then barked some more.

Gia looked up.

Sure enough, Rocky Raccoon lounged on a low branch, one front paw tucked beneath his chin, the other three paws hanging lazily over the branch as he watched the group. Gia was pretty sure he was smirking.

A quick glance at the garbage covering the top of her pail told her they'd most likely interrupted his meal. So much for the trapper. First thing tomorrow, she was calling and demanding her six hundred dollars back.

On the bright side, there was no sign of the bear. Still . . . "Come on in. Let me just get Thor fed, and —"

"Oh, he and Brandy ate before we left the store. I wanted to get them taken care of before the storms," Zoe said.

Pushing all thoughts of wildlife out of her mind, Gia started toward the door with her friends. At the sound of another car pulling into the driveway, she stopped and waved.

Alfie bounded out of the car and across the lawn. "Hey, Gia. Thanks for the text. I can't wait to get back into this."

"Sure thing." She opened the door, then waited for them to precede her. The aroma of the pizza Cole must have put in the oven overwhelmed her the minute she stepped into the kitchen. Her stomach growled. With seven of them already there, and Hunt and Leo on their way, it didn't make sense to try to sit in the small kitchen. Instead, she set up a buffet on the table. As long as they took Thor, Klondike, and Brandy into the living room with them, it should work.

Once everyone was settled with pizza, sodas, and a few bowls of chips Savannah set out on the coffee table, they discussed everything but murder, enjoying the mo-

273

ment with friends before turning to more somber subjects.

The cozy house wasn't exactly spacious, and with her, Savannah, Cole, Cybil, Alfie, Trevor, and Zoe, plus Thor and Brandy sprawled on the floor, Klondike lounging on the back of Gia's seat, and Hunt and Leo supposedly trying to stop by, it was definitely crowded, but in a good way.

Gia had been a loner when she was married, spending most of her home time alone, which was part of the reason she'd kept her job in the busy deli that had readied her for the café. She'd fled New York to escape — scared, alone, insecure. Though she knew she'd have Savannah, who'd already been her only close friend but had returned to Florida before Gia had married Bradley, she'd never even dreamed of a house filled with so much love, laughter, and family. And a dog! For the first time in her life, she shared her very own home with a pet. Tears threatened as she looked around the room and started to choke up.

Anticipating her thoughts, as usual, Savannah caught her gaze and smiled, then shot Gia her best "I told you so" smirk.

Gia couldn't help but smile. Everything in her life was so perfect. Except for this murder investigation hanging over them. It was time to get it off their plates so they could move on with happier times. Needing a moment to compose herself, Gia stood and grabbed the Post-it pad Alfie had jotted down the camera notes on, then got a legal pad from her desk. With so many people present, it would be easier to jot the notes on the pad than try to pull out a laptop. She could always transfer them to a document later.

"Okay. First things first. Alfie, can you show everyone the security footage?"

"Sure thing." He pulled his phone out of his pocket, scrolled and tapped, and handed it first to Zoe beside him. "I put together clips in order of appearance, beginning with Officer Erickson at four forty-five, and emailed it to myself so everyone could take a look."

When Zoe was finished, she passed the phone to Trevor.

Tucking her legs beneath her, Gia munched on barbeque chips and waited until everyone had seen the video. She balanced the pad on her lap, set Alfie's list atop it, and tapped the pen. A moment later, she laughed at herself, realizing she must have picked up the tapping habit from Savannah and Hunt — a habit that drove Gia crazy — and stilled her hand. After taking the phone from Cybil and reviewing the footage once more herself, Gia handed Alfie's phone back. "Why don't we start with the timeline from the camera footage, then try to see who has motive, opportunity, and an alibi."

Savannah lifted her slice of pizza, cheese oozing off onto her plate. "Why don't we start with Amanda. She was in the forest at what time?"

Gia squinted to make out Alfie's chicken scratch. "Seven twenty-eight."

"So, about a half hour before Rusty was killed." Savannah set her plate on the coffee table and sipped her Diet Coke. "That would have been plenty of time to get from — which camera picked her up?"

"The grocery store."

She closed her eyes, traced an imaginary map in the air with one glitter-tipped blue nail. "More than enough time to get from point A, where the camera picked her up, into the parking lot, then walk to where Rusty was found."

"I don't know." Moving on the forest floor, even on the well-beaten trails, was not the same as walking down the sidewalk. It was slightly rougher terrain, and roots stuck up in places, not to mention the critters you had to watch out for — or maybe that was just Gia. "I think that would be cutting it kind of close."

"Nah." Savannah's eyes popped open, and she returned to her pizza. "A brisk pace would be enough. And if she was headed there to kill her husband, chances are her stride would have been determined. My money's on her."

"Yeah?" Gia wasn't convinced. "Even if you're right, and the woman was cheating on her husband, there's a huge leap from infidelity to murder. Especially killing someone you'd been intimate with — that would take a special kind of cold."

"Or the heat of passion." Setting her plate back in her lap, Savannah ticked points off on her fingers. "One, she had opportunity, because she was in the forest with a reasonable amount of time to have committed the crime, even if she had to run to get to him on time. Two, she had motive. Of course, anyone who'd ever met that man probably had motive, but still, she had to live with him. And if she divorced him, or he divorced her, as Ariyah suggested, she risked having to pay him alimony or share part of her vast fortune with a man she admittedly despised."

"I can't argue that." Gia tried to envision the woman she'd met hightailing it through the forest, gun in hand, stalking her husband with the intention of killing him. It wasn't a pretty picture, but not one she could completely discount either.

But Savannah wouldn't be deterred. "And three, she may or may not have an alibi, because even if Caleb Ryan was her lover, and even if he vouched for her, what's to say he's telling the truth when he stands to gain at least one business that he obviously wanted and perhaps Rusty's wife as well?"

Good point. "Okay, that brings us to suspect number two. Caleb Ryan. You just established he had motive, we know he went into the forest five minutes after Amanda, so were the two meeting for a lovers' tryst, and just so happened to choose the spot Amanda's husband was about to be murdered in?"

Trevor shook his head. "No way. That's just too coincidental."

Zoe nodded her agreement. "What are the chances of that happening?"

"Probably no more than one in a million," Gia said.

"At best," Alfie added around a bit of pizza. "Probably much slimmer."

"But you have to admit, he has motive and opportunity, and his alibi is flimsy at best." Cybil glanced at Cole before continuing, then winced as she forged on. "Maybe Caleb and Amanda conspired to kill him together and frame Cole for it. Amanda told you she blamed Cole for leaving her to that monster. What better way to get revenge? Because in addition to motive and opportunity, you are probably looking for someone who harbored enough animosity toward Cole to frame him for murder and ruin the rest of his life."

Even the mouthful she took of her Diet Coke couldn't wash down the lump in Gia's throat. What if it did turn out to be Amanda? Would Cole be able to get past that? She glanced at him, his fingers entwined with Cybil's. It might not be easy, but together they'd make it. He'd have to.

Gia wrote down Amanda and Caleb's names, then drew columns and added their motives and opportunities. Under each of their alibi columns she put the other's name with a question mark. Flimsy was right. "How do you feel about Caleb and Brynleigh Colton as our Bonnie and Clyde?"

"The woman from the zoning commission?" Zoe asked. "I remember working with her when I got the permits for the doggy daycare. She seemed competent enough. Why do you suspect her?"

"I guess I don't really." Gia jotted down

279

her name anyway. "But she did appear to be arguing with Caleb today, and I just can't imagine why the business license for the bakery was issued the day after Rusty was killed, and the contract selling the shop to Caleb was signed on the day of his murder. Especially when Rusty supposedly bribed her to squash Caleb's permits, allowing Rusty to sweep in and grab the building."

"Which Amanda would have had to been involved in," Savannah argued.

"True." She jotted down the names together with a question mark. She'd need more to go on than she had if she wanted to put Brynleigh on the list. Right now, she barely had any kind of motive, and no opportunity, since Brynleigh wasn't seen on any of the security camera footage — which didn't mean she hadn't found another way in, but still . . . And as far as an alibi, for all they knew she could have been in a roomful of people at the time. But someone else did have opportunity. On the next line, she wrote Ariyah O'Neil. "I think I'm leaning toward Ariyah."

Savannah frowned and scooted closer to the edge of her seat on the love seat. "Why Ariyah?"

Gia shrugged. She wasn't really sure what made her lean that way, but the woman just didn't strike her as genuine. She glanced at the time Ariyah had passed the bar camera — two minutes after Rusty — and froze. She lurched up straighter. "Because she lied."

Cole leaned forward too. "Lied about what?"

"When she came to see me in the café, which I found odd to begin with, she said she saw Amanda leave the hotel ten minutes after Rusty did, but she couldn't have."

"Because she would have had to leave a minute or two after him to have been so close on his tail when he passed the camera." Savannah jumped up and rounded the table to sit beside Gia on the couch so she could look over her shoulder at the paper. "So, she had opportunity. But what was her motive?"

"She also said Rusty was cheating with Brynleigh Colton, claimed she was okay with it and loved him anyway, but maybe she got tired of sharing." Gia jotted down the information. "But why come into the café and say anything if she's guilty?"

Trevor shot to his feet. "To establish an alibi."

"Huh? How could I be her alibi that far after the killing?"

He started to pace, stepping over Brandy

281

then Thor with each circuit. "Think about it. You just happen to be engaged to the investigator in charge of the case and best friends with his partner's wife, which wouldn't be difficult to find out, not if you were in Boggy Creek for more than five minutes."

She couldn't argue that, and it wouldn't be the first time she'd ended up in a jam over being close with Hunt, Savannah, and Leo.

"Plus, she stepped forward of her own accord to let you know she was still at the hotel ten minutes after Rusty left, which she wasn't, and for the icing on the cake, she cast blame on someone else, Amanda, for committing the crime." In his excitement, he missed stepping over Brandy, tripped, and sprawled face-first onto the rug. Without missing a beat, he held up a finger. "My bet's on her."

Gia set the pad aside to help him up, since she was the closest. "You okay?"

"Yeah." He petted Brandy's head. "Sorry, girl. I guess I got a little overzealous."

Gia laughed and returned to her seat, the moment of levity needed but too short.

Cole cleared his throat. "As much as it absolutely pains me to say this, what about Jim Kirkman?"

Gia had thought of that earlier. "He definitely had motive, though he's waited an awfully long time to seek revenge if that was the case."

"But no one has spoken to him. For all we know, Rusty could have recently contacted him, just to rub it in his face and gloat." Cole clenched his fist, and Cybil yanked her hand back. "Oh, sorry, babe. You okay?"

She held her hand back out to him, and he took it. "I'm fine."

"That would have been just like Rusty." Cole shook his head, clearly pained by the possibility. "So we have to at least consider he had motive."

"As far as opportunity, though, we have no idea. Just because Savannah and I couldn't find him doesn't mean he wasn't in Orlando at the time of the murder," Gia argued. No way did she want to believe it was him, to see him spend the rest of his life in prison after all he'd already been through.

"And who's to say he doesn't have an alibi for the time in question?" It seemed Savannah agreed with Gia it was a long shot. Or maybe they both just really wanted a happily ever after for him and Rhonda when this was all said and done. "Okay, so I feel like we need to talk to Amanda and Ariyah again and then find Jim."

"I'll tell you what, Gia." Cole lifted Cybil's hand, kissed her knuckles. "I'll open in the morning, and you can go to the hotel and question Amanda and Ariyah, then you can take over after lunch, and I'll go see if I can find Jim."

"You sure, Cole?"

"I am." He nodded, his face red, whether from anger or embarrassment, she couldn't tell. "I was planning to look for him anyway, and if there's any chance he's the killer, I don't want you or Savannah anywhere near him."

"Okay." Not wanting to upset him any further, Gia let it go. "So, what questions does that leave us with?"

Savannah tapped Alfie's list. "We still don't know who drove the rental car that passed the camera that morning, or if it had anything to do with Rusty's death."

"Huh." Gia scribbled *rental car* at the bottom of the list, followed by *passenger* and a question mark. "We also weren't able to say for certain whether or not Rusty was alone in the car when he passed by the bar. Did anyone happen to notice if either of the women in the videos was wearing a hat?"

They all shook their heads, and Alfie

pulled up the footage and watched again. "Nope. Neither has a hat on. Why?"

"Harley said he saw a lady wearing a hat in the forest that morning while he was washing the poison ivy off his arms."

"I'll tell you what . . ." Alfie tucked the phone back into his pocket. "I'll run a search later, see if I can find any other security cameras in the area I might be able to tap into, then let you know."

"Great, thanks." Gia made notes of everything they had to follow up on — the rental car, Rusty's possible passenger, Jim's whereabouts, and a lady in a hat.

"There's something else bothering me." Cybil had been mostly quiet until then, but she turned to Cole and addressed him directly. "If someone was trying to frame you, and I'm assuming that's the case between the receipt with the meeting time found with Rusty and the weapon found at the café, how did whoever set it up know you'd be in the forest that morning? Seems like an awfully big risk to leave that to chance."

His eyes widened, and he lurched to his feet. "Son of a —" Then he yanked his phone from his pocket as he stalked toward the kitchen.

Cybil caught her bottom lip between her

285

teeth and looked around the room at everyone staring at her for answers. "We've been meeting early in the mornings and walking in that same general area for about a month now, since it's close to my house and Cole can't go too far if he's going to make it to work on time."

"But the only way someone could know that . . ." Gia's blood ran cold.

Savannah finished, "Is if the killer had been following you, or more likely, Cole."

CHAPTER TWENTY-THREE

While the implications of Cole possibly being stalked by a killer sank in, a somber hush descended until Cole returned and said Hunt and Leo would be there in a few minutes.

Alfie finally broke the silence. "You know, there's someone else you're forgetting to include on that list."

Gia ran through the names. "Amanda, Caleb, Ariyah, and Jim. Brynleigh, I suppose, even if we can't place her in the forest. Who'd I miss?"

"Officer Erickson."

Gia chuckled. "He's a police officer."

Alfie held up his hand. "I know, but just hear me out. He was on camera entering the forest early that morning."

"Probably to go to work," Gia argued.

"Still . . . he was somewhere in that forest at the time Rusty was killed, so he had opportunity. Plus, he was the first police officer on the scene."

"Which isn't all that unusual when a crime is committed on park land," Savannah pointed out.

"I'm just saying, he was the one to find the receipt with the meeting time, and he was also first on the scene when someone broke into the café and planted the gun."

"Hmm." Gia looked at Savannah. "And that is unusual. What are the chances he just happened to be driving past the café in the middle of the night within the minute or so after I realized someone had broken in? Especially if he was on his way into the forest at quarter to five in the morning, since that rules out him working the night shift."

Cole still stood near the doorway. "First, does anyone want anything else before I sit?"

Gia couldn't eat another bite, and even if she hadn't been stuffed before, which she had been, the thought of a killer keeping tabs on Cole, and therefore noting all of their comings and goings at the café and possibly Cybil's at home, would have ruined her appetite.

After they all declined, Cole returned to his seat beside Cybil. "Okay, second, it's very reasonable to expect Officer Erickson would have worked that late after a murder was committed on his shift and he was first on the scene. I'm sure he had a pile of paperwork a mile high. Think about it, Gia, after you spoke to Hunt at the scene, when did you next see him?"

"Touché." Gia had been with Hunt long enough, and through more than a few murder investigations, to know whatever shift you were assigned to flew out the window in the midst of an investigation. "Besides, he doesn't appear to have any motive we know of or any connection to Rusty or Cole . . ."

He shook his head when she glanced at him. "I'd never met him before that morning."

Still, she added his name anyway. May as well have all of the players on one list. You never knew what might jump out at you seeing them all together. "I'm just thinking about the receipt. We still haven't figured out who bought the blueberry muffins."

"Because, theoretically, it was more than likely the killer or an accomplice who made the purchase." Savannah lifted a brow at Gia. "And who had blueberry muffins in a room she didn't share with her husband?"

"Point taken." Gia added the information, the page now so overcrowded she could barely make sense of it all. "I'll ask Amanda about it in the morning."

"That's fine," Savannah agreed. "But I'm going with you. Willow and Skyla will be fine until we get there."

"And Earl's always around in the mornings," Cole added. "I'll ask him if he can hang out until you guys get back, just in case we need the help."

Headlights blared through the front window and washed along the wall, casting reflections through the raindrops and condensation clinging to the window, interrupting any further discussion.

When the front door opened and Hunt walked in, Gia's heart tripped. It still amazed her that she'd been able to fall so head-over-heels in love with him after what Bradley had put her through. And it astonished her even more that Hunt had been so patient with her trust issues, had waited to ask her to marry him until he'd known for sure Gia had learned to trust and believe in him. She threw her arms around his neck, lay her cheek against his chest, and spent one moment enjoying the warmth of his embrace, the woodsy scent of his aftershave, the steady beat of his heart.

He stepped back too soon, gripped her shoulders, and studied her. "You okay?"

"I am, yes." She offered a smile. "Just missed you is all."

"Yeah?" His grin turned instantly cocky, and he tugged a strand of her hair. "I missed you too."

Heat rushed up her face, and she stepped back. "Come in and eat something, since I already know you probably haven't all day."

He offered a hello to everyone as he petted Thor, Klondike, and Brandy, then slung an arm around her shoulder.

"Hey, Leo," she called as she led Hunt to the kitchen.

He grabbed two plates and loaded a couple of slices on each while Gia poured sodas for him and Leo. "You want me to throw those slices in the oven?"

"Nah. We'll be happy if we get to shovel them down before we have to run out over one thing or another." He paused, frowned at her. "Besides, I have to question all of you over Cole's allegations that he thinks the killer may have been following him."

She nodded, more than a little spooked by the idea.

"But we can take a few minutes to say hi and catch up before the interrogation begins," he said.

"Good." She grinned. "Because you're just in time."

"Oh?" He picked up the plates, propped one on his arm to grab a stack of napkins, and waited. "Just in time for what, exactly?"

"We were just finishing up, and then we were about to solve your case for you."

A laugh blurted out, and he almost dropped the plate he was balancing. "Oh, really?"

"Yup."

"Can't wait to see this."

She grinned and shoved the door to the living room open then held it for him. She lifted onto her tiptoes and kissed his cheek as he passed. "But since you and Leo are here anyway, feel free to help."

He just shook his head, handed Leo a plate, and sat, then groaned as he simply held the plate in his lap and let his head fall back against the couch cushion and closed his eyes. "Good thing you're planning on picking up the slack on this one. I'm exhausted."

Leo's hand stopped midway to his mouth. "What?"

Hunt grinned and sat up. "Savannah didn't tell you? These guys are about to solve our homicide."

To his credit, Leo leveled Savannah a sideways glance, and a smile played at the corner of his mouth, but he didn't laugh.

He probably knew better. Laughing at her would only make Savannah dig in, be more likely to prove she could do it.

Hunt had no such inhibitions, and his eyes lit with humor as he winked at his cousin.

Being the mature, sophisticated woman she was, Savannah stuck her tongue out at him.

After checking that everyone had what they needed and were comfortably seated around the coffee table, Gia settled beside Hunt on the couch. "I don't suppose you guys found the killer yet, right?"

He swallowed and wiped his mouth. "No."

She had no doubt he wouldn't lie to her about that, but . . . "Would you have told me if you had?"

"Probably not until after I heard your theories." He shot her a mischievous grin but sobered much too quickly. "As it is, we have a killer on the loose in Boggy Creek, and while we believe Rusty was the specific target, we can't say for sure."

Silence descended for a moment while they all digested that. The possibility that Rusty hadn't been targeted specifically, but rather had been convenient when the killer struck, hadn't occurred to Gia. Somehow, the thought was way more terrifying. Before, she'd been concerned with absolving Cole.

Now it was time to focus on finding the killer, because they were all potentially in danger until they did. Especially when all of them enjoyed hiking and kayaking in the forest. "Do you think it's still safe in the forest?"

"I honestly don't know." He shook his head, then pinned them one by one with his gaze.

"But I wouldn't mind if all of you stayed out of there until we have this guy behind bars."

"Do you have any suspects?" Cole asked.

Hunt shrugged and downed a mouthful of lukewarm pizza.

Gia never had developed a taste for cold pizza — she enjoyed hers hot and steamy, right out of the oven, with long stretches of melted mozzarella. Her stomach growled at the thought. How could she possibly be hungry again? She couldn't, and stress eating wouldn't help anything. "Did you guys find Rusty's car?"

"Yeah, in the lot closest to the crime scene."

Gia nodded. "That would make sense considering he drove in on the road that went past the bar."

Hunt stopped mid-bite, eyes wide, and stared at her.

Savannah laughed out loud. "You thought she was kidding about solving your case?"

He set his slice deliberately back on his plate. "How do you know that?"

"I might have, uh . . ." Oops. She purposely kept her gaze from shifting to Alfie, but caught his posture stiffening in her peripheral vision.

Hunt held up a hand. "You know what? Forget it. For now."

"That's probably for the best." She offered her sweetest smile, a trick she'd learned from Savannah when dealing with Hunt. "Maybe it would be best if you asked the questions."

"Uh-huh." He took a drink before turning to Cole. "You said on the phone you were afraid the killer had been stalking you. What makes you think that?"

He shifted to face Hunt more fully. "Because how else would he have known I'd be in the forest that morning?"

Hunt nodded thoughtfully, took another bite, and swallowed. "Did you notice anyone following you in the days before Rusty came into the café?"

"No. I didn't notice anything out of the ordinary."

"Did you see anyone in particular during your walks? Maybe the same person hanging out in the forest? Someone you'd never noticed before that you suddenly seemed to bump into everywhere?"

He glanced at Cybil, then shook his head.

"But we don't always walk on the trails either," Cybil said. She'd been hiking that forest forever, and she loved nature, often straying from the marked trails to wander through the more natural settings.

"Okay, while I agree it would be too big a coincidence for you to be the one to stumble onto Rusty's body if the killer hadn't tracked your movements, the setup would still have worked even if someone else had come across the body. The receipt with your name, number, and meeting time still would have been found. The weapon, which, by the way, did match the one used to kill Rusty, could still have been planted in the café, and Leo would still have found the business card in Gia's back parking lot. It was just a bonus that you found his body as well."

Gia wasn't sure if that brought any relief — possibly some. "So, as long as the killer knew Cole occasionally walked that area, and could possibly have been sighted by someone at one time or another, that might have been enough?"

"Exactly." Hunt's phone dinged a notification, and he pulled it out of his pocket, then paused. "It's possible he or she followed Cole once or twice but didn't necessarily have to stalk him on a regular basis."

That, at least, eased her mind a little. But they'd all do well to steer clear of the forest for the foreseeable future.

Hunt checked his phone, then shoved to his feet and set his second slice on the coffee table. "Leo, we have to go."

"What's up?" He kissed Savannah's cheek and stood, setting his plate on the table but taking his second slice with him.

"We may have just caught a break."

Gia walked him to the door, Savannah and Leo alongside them. When Gia opened the door, Hunt paused.

He pointed a finger back and forth between Gia and Savannah. "And you two, stay out of trouble."

Savannah eased the door shut behind them, then turned to lean her back against the door. "So, are we going to? Stay out of trouble, I mean?"

Gia only shrugged. "Probably not."

CHAPTER TWENTY-FOUR

Instead of dealing with valet parking, Gia pulled into the hotel lot the next morning and hopped out of the car. She waited for Savannah to get out, then locked the car and pocketed her key. "Who do you want to start with, Ariyah or Amanda?"

"Let's talk to Ariyah first." Savannah held a pack of gum out for Gia to take a piece, then popped a piece into her own mouth and dropped the pack back into her bag. "At least that way if we want to follow up with Amanda on anything Ariyah has to say, we can. I have a feeling we'll be lucky to get even one shot at talking to her. No way she'll see us again afterward."

"True." Gia pulled the door open, held it for Savannah, then followed her inside. Since they already knew the room numbers, they skipped the receptionist and headed straight for the elevator. "You think maybe we should try good cop, bad cop with

Amanda?"

Savannah laughed as they entered the elevator. "If only Hunt could see you now."

"Right." Gia pushed the button for three, then watched the numbers ding up.

"I suppose you want me to be the good cop?" Savannah asked.

"No way." She'd seen Savannah figuratively rip someone to shreds without ever raising her voice or losing her smile. "You're better at bad cop than I am."

"Glad you know it." She strode from the elevator and straight to Ariyah's door.

Gia checked her watch then knocked. "You don't think it's too early, do you?"

Savannah shrugged. "Too late now if it is."

"I guess." Gia wiped her sweat-slicked palms on her leggings. What did she have to be nervous about? Nothing. Ariyah had approached her first, so it was perfectly reasonable she'd follow up if she had questions.

A man wearing a white terry-cloth robe with the hotel logo emblazoned on the lapel opened the door. "Can I help you ladies?"

"I'm sorry." Gia checked the room number, looked over her shoulder at Amanda's room across the hall. "I'm looking for Ariyah O'Neil."

"You must have the wrong room."

Or she'd already left. "Can you tell me when you checked in?"

"Late last night. We were supposed to arrive this morning, but we beat traffic all the way down 95."

"Honey, who's at the door?" A woman dressed in shorts and a Florida T-shirt, holding a yogurt-covered toddler on her hip, peeked out over his shoulder.

"I'm sorry to bother you, ma'am." Gia smiled at the grinning toddler. "We were looking for a friend who was staying in this room."

"Oh." She winced as the baby tugged on her hair. "She must have checked out yesterday. When we arrived last night, the receptionist said they had a room free because a guest checked out early."

"Thank you for your help. Sorry to have bothered you."

"No bother at all." The woman stepped back, and the man closed the door behind her.

"Huh." Gia leaned against the wall, arms folded. "What do you make of that?"

Savannah shrugged it off. "With Rusty gone, assuming she was only here to spend time with him, it makes sense she'd go home."

"I guess." But still, Gia would have expected her to hang around for at least a day or two in case the police had any further questions. If she wasn't guilty, that is. "You'd think she might wait to see if they figured out who killed him."

"Maybe," Savannah said. "But it could also be Rusty was paying for the room, and with him gone, she might get stuck with the bill."

"I hadn't thought of that." But it was possible, though she doubted it if Amanda was the one footing the bill for the rooms, which from everything they'd learned was probably the case. In Gia's mind, taking off this early in the investigation pointed even more to Ariyah's guilt. But, since there was nothing they could do about it at the moment, she strode across the hallway and knocked on Amanda's door. "Let's just hope Amanda's still here."

Amanda swung the door open, then rolled her eyes.

Since the door had a peephole she should have looked through before opening it, Gia figured the gesture was meant for effect. Therefore, she ignored it. "Good morning, Mrs. Bragge. I was wondering if you have a few minutes. There were a couple of questions I wanted to ask you."

She stepped back from the door and

gestured them in with a flourish. "Might as well call me Amanda if you're going to keep on stopping by like we're old friends or something. Drink?"

At nine a.m.? Thankfully, Gia bit the comment back before it could slip out.

"Starting early, huh?" Savannah smiled and batted her long lashes once. "I guess murder'll do that to you."

"Yup." She poured a drink then flopped onto the bed with it, back against the headboard, one ankle crossed over the other. She gestured toward the two chairs, probably about as close to an offer to sit as they were going to get.

The same number of muffins that had been there on their previous visit still sat in the basket in the center of the table, no doubt stale by now. "Where'd you get the muffins?"

"No idea." She waved it off. "They were a gift from some business associate of Rusty's."

"Why didn't Rusty's business associate send them to Rusty's room instead of yours?" Uh-oh. Savannah might be taking bad cop a little too far.

"He didn't. He sent them to Rusty, then Rusty brought them in here to share." She took a long swallow of her drink. "Is there a problem with that?"

"No, ma'am, I'm just insatiably curious." Savannah shot her a killer smile.

"Right. Well." Another drink drained the glass, and she set it aside on the nightstand. "Well, if that's all you came to ask —"

"Amanda . . ." Gia interrupted before Savannah could say anything else. "You already know we're trying to exonerate Cole, and no matter what went on between the two of you and how you feel about him now, you can't possibly want him to get convicted of a murder he didn't commit."

"If for no other reason," Savannah added, "wouldn't you want the person who actually killed your husband to be found and punished accordingly?"

Her expression softened. "Oh, I don't hate Cole. I don't even have any real animosity toward him. After walking in on Rusty and me, I don't even blame him for walking away. I might have done the same."

"And yet, when it was Rusty doing the cheating, you didn't," Gia said softly.

"No. No, I guess I didn't. And it's not like I didn't know he was cheating on me, I've known for years, but as long as he was wrapped up with his hussies, he left me alone." She stood, picked up her glass, and went to the bar, then set the glass down and turned without refilling it. "Rusty was one of those men who had a casual relationship with the truth, if you know what I mean."

"I know the type. If his lips are moving, he's lyin'," Savannah said with a sympathetic cluck.

"Exactly. So, I never believed a word he said. The man was a liar, and a cheat, and a scammer, and yet . . ." She shivered and wrapped her arms around herself. "He didn't deserve to end up dead in the woods, stuffed under a tangle of roots like a bag of garbage."

Alarm bells clanged in Gia's head, and she desperately sought to school her expression to keep from reacting. Besides, there were other ways Amanda could have found out how her husband had been found without her having been the one to dump him there. For all she knew, Hunt could have shown her pictures of the crime scene. "What were you doing in the forest the morning Rusty was killed?"

If the question rattled her, she gave no outward sign other than a sigh. "I met up with a friend for an early-morning walk. Not like there's anything else to do in Podunk."

"Caleb Ryan?" Gia asked.

"What?" She screwed up her expression. "No. Brynleigh Colton."

"Bryn . . ." She looked to Savannah for a reaction but got none. "You're friends with Brynleigh?"

"Yup. Been friends for years."

"But wasn't she . . ."

"Sleeping with my husband? Yes." She shrugged. "But as I've already stated, I didn't care."

Gia massaged the back of her neck, where tension had settled and begun to throb. "So you were meeting Brynleigh to go for a walk in the woods right when and where your husband was murdered? And you didn't see anything?"

"I didn't see him get killed, if that's what you're asking."

"Did you know he planned to go to the forest that morning?"

She seemed to weigh her words before answering. "He may have mentioned it."

That was new. Gia thought of the possibility of a passenger in his car. "Might he have mentioned going with or meeting anyone there?"

She clammed up, turned, and poured another drink.

All right. Maybe she should change the subject before Amanda got tired of answering questions and tossed them out. "Were you aware that Rusty bribed Brynleigh to

305

get the shop?"

She shrugged. "Of course I was. Who do you think paid her?"

Gia's head whirled. Savannah seemed to have forgotten her role and deferred to Gia to ask the next questions, but she couldn't sort through the confusion to decide what else to ask. She turned her attention to Savannah and willed her to come up with something.

Apparently getting the message, Savannah sat up straighter. "You weren't by chance wearing a hat in the forest that morning, were you?"

Gia shot her a *what are you talking about* look, but Savannah simply shrugged, a barely perceptible lift of her shoulder with an apologetic expression.

Amanda stared at her for a moment, then answered. "No, but Brynleigh was. Does that matter?"

"Nah, just wondered." Savannah pointed up toward the ceiling. "Sun here can get pretty brutal, even that early in the morning. Can't be too careful out there."

"Uh, thanks for the advice. I'll keep that in mind." She frowned. "You do know we actually live in Florida, right? It just made more sense to stay at the hotel until our business was completed than it did to drive back and forth."

"Oh, right." Savannah glanced at Gia and tilted her head just a bit, tossing the ball to her court.

"Did Brynleigh ride with you out to the forest?"

"No. She met me out there."

"In a rental car?" Gia held her breath.

"Yeah."

Bingo. At least she'd found out something from this conversation that made sense. But if Brynleigh was driving the rental car, who could have potentially been riding with Rusty? All of their current suspects were now accounted for. And they could put every one of them in the forest that morning, so all of them now had opportunity. Maybe the shadow in Rusty's passenger seat had been nothing more than a reflection after all.

Her mind raced through the list. If Brynleigh and Amanda were together — conveniently perhaps? In order to alibi one another? — what was Caleb doing there? She'd assumed he'd been with Amanda. And what did that do for her suspicions? Did it change anything? Maybe. She'd assumed Amanda would alibi Caleb. The fact that she hadn't meant that Caleb now had no alibi at all, flimsy or otherwise. "Did the muffins happen to come with a receipt or a card?"

"Not that I saw." But she didn't question why Gia was asking about the muffins again.

As far as Gia was concerned, that kept her high on the suspect list. Probably. Maybe she just didn't care.

Gia stood. She needed time to update her list, sort through everything they'd learned, and figure out how the puzzle pieces fit together. "Thank you for your time, Amanda. We'll get in touch again if we have any more questions."

"I'm sure you will."

Gia ignored the smart retort and smiled as she bid her goodbye. She and Savannah remained quiet as they walked down the hallway, Gia lost in her own thoughts.

When Savannah stopped in front of the elevator, she looked back over her shoulder and frowned.

"Something wrong?"

"Just the little hairs on the back of my neck standing at attention. I hate that feeling."

"Did you see anyone?"

"Nope." But she still kept scanning the area.

Gia pushed the button for the lobby and

waited. "Okay, so we know Brynleigh was driving the rental car."

"And we know Brynleigh was the woman Harley saw wearing the hat."

"If she's telling the truth," Gia said.

"Right."

"And we know someone sent the muffins to them."

"Supposedly."

"Fine. Supposedly." The elevator door opened and they stepped inside. "Do you think it's possible the killer isn't on our list?"

Savannah frowned. "I guess anything's possible, but —"

Just as the doors shut, the unmistakable *pop, pop* of gunfire erupted from the hallway.

She jammed the button for the doors to open, but the elevator had already started its descent. "Call Hunt or wait?"

Savannah practically vibrated with nervous energy as she yanked out her phone. "Better safe than sorry."

Gia held her breath when the elevator doors opened into the lobby, then quickly pushed the three button repeatedly — as if that would make the doors close any faster.

Savannah relayed the information to Hunt.

When the doors finally opened enough on the third floor, Gia bolted through and sprinted down the hallway. She found Amanda lying in the doorway, blood gushing from her chest. Gia dropped to her knees and pressed her hand against the wound. "Oh, no. Oh, no. Oh, no."

Savannah hurtled over her, grabbed a towel off the bed and tossed it to Gia. Then she dropped on Amanda's other side and pressed her fingers against her throat to feel for a pulse.

CHAPTER TWENTY-FIVE

Hours after they'd found Amanda, Savannah walked into the café kitchen. "You almost ready to go?"

"Just about." Gia finished wrapping the bowl of peppers and onions she'd just cut up for the morning.

"Everything out front is done, and the front door is locked, so we can just go out the back whenever you're ready." Resigned to waiting a few more minutes to head home, after an exhausting day, Savannah pulled out a stool from the island and plopped down, elbow on the counter, chin resting in her hand. "Leo just called from the hospital."

Gia froze, one hand on the refrigerator handle, bracing herself for the news that Amanda hadn't made it.

"It's all right, Gia. She's out of surgery, and they expect her to make a full recovery." She blew out a breath. "Thank God we were right there when it happened. They're saying the only reason she survived was the immediate first aid she received on the scene."

Relief rushed through Gia, leaving her even more weary than she'd been moments before. Her legs turned to rubber, and she stuck the bowl in the fridge, then slumped down across from Savannah. "Did he say anything else? Were they able to question her?"

Savannah was already shaking her head. "She's still in recovery, hasn't fully come out of the anesthesia yet, but the doctors are optimistic she may wake up enough tonight to at least tell them who shot her."

"Do you think she knows?" And was it the same person who'd killed Rusty?

Savannah shrugged, tracing circles on the counter with her nail. "I don't see how she couldn't. To have shot her in the chest at what they say was close range, she'd have had to be face-to-face with her attacker."

"So unless he or she was wearing a mask . . ."

"She knows who did it."

Gia sighed, massaging the bridge of her nose between a thumb and forefinger. Maybe she'd just sit there all night, fall asleep with her head on the counter. Or they could ask Zoe to stop by and take care of Thor, Klondike, and Pepper, and she and Savannah could crash in the apartment upstairs. Theoretically, she could be face-down on the semi-comfortable couch in a minute or less, instead of dropping Savannah off, making the twenty-minute trek home, then tending to Thor and Klondike, and possibly picking up garbage the raccoon shredded across her lawn, while keeping one eye out in every direction for bears.

As tempting as the idea was, she needed to go home. Even more than sleep, she needed to curl up with Thor and Klondike and have peace for a little while. Even if it was only an illusion. Hopefully, it would at least last until morning.

Savannah tapped her nail against the counter. "Do you think whoever shot Amanda was the same person who killed Rusty?"

"I don't know. It seems likely, but for what purpose? None of the suspects or motives we came up with pointed toward Amanda as a potential victim." A fact that had gnawed at Gia relentlessly ever since they'd found her unconscious and covered in blood. Could the attempt on her life have been prevented if they'd figured something out sooner? A detail that weighed heavily on Hunt, since he'd admitted as much earlier. But no matter how many times she ran through different scenarios, she couldn't see a connection.

"I have another theory," Savannah said.

"Yeah?"

"What if Amanda did kill Rusty, and someone shot her in retaliation?"

Huh. That was a possibility she hadn't explored. "But who?"

Savannah sucked in a deep breath and let it out slowly. "Ariyah?"

Wow. That made a sick sort of sense. "I guess it's possible. Considering Hunt has the gun that was used to kill Rusty in evidence, whoever it was had to have used another weapon. I suppose it could be another killer too."

Savannah opened her mouth to say something, then snapped it closed at the sound of the front door opening, followed by footsteps.

Gia lunged for the rack on the counter, yanked a butcher knife from the holder, and held it tucked low behind her leg.

Savannah grabbed the rolling pin from the drying rack and stepped to the side of the door, where she'd be invisible if it opened.

With the lights in the kitchen still on, and those in the dining room turned off, she didn't bother exposing herself to whomever might be there by peeking out. Instead, she steered clear of the cutout and waited. She held her breath. The ringing in her ears drowned out all other sound.

The door to the kitchen eased open, and Savannah lunged, rolling pin raised.

"Whoa!" Cole staggered back through the doorway into the hall. "Yo, hey, it's just me."

Savannah tossed the rolling pin aside and pressed a hand against her chest. She bent at the waist, braced both hands on her knees, and sucked in deep breaths.

After returning the knife to its place, Gia lay a hand on Savannah's back. With the other hand, she gently gripped her shoulder, eased her up, and guided her back to the stool where she'd been sitting. "You okay?"

"Yeah." She breathed in deeply, shaky. "Sorry. Sometimes I'm still easily spooked."

Cole wrapped an arm around her shoulders, pulled her against him. "I'm so sorry, honey. I didn't mean to startled you."

She patted Cole's hand, then turned her hand over and weaved her fingers between Gia's. "It's okay. Really. I promise, I'm fine."

"Are you still getting panic attacks?"

She lowered her gaze and nodded. "But they're far less frequent, and the therapist is helping a lot. So . . ."

Gia stepped back to give her some breathing room, and Cole sat beside her.

Savannah pinned him with a glare. "As long as people don't sneak up on me when there's a killer on the loose, I'm doing pretty good."

Cole winced.

"I'm just messing with you, sweetie." She winked. "I ain't that fragile."

"No, you're not." Cole looked her straight in the eye. "You're one of the strongest women I know."

She smiled, tears shimmering in her thick lashes, turning her eyes an even more brilliant blue. "Thank you for that. And now, if you're finished scaring me half to death, and if you've locked the front door . . ."

He nodded.

"Did you find Jim Kirkman?"

Gia held her breath. If Cole had found him, it meant he couldn't have shot Amanda, though he still could have killed Rusty. She resisted the urge to cross her fingers.

"I found him."

She released the breath slowly, then stood and went to the fridge, pulled out three bottles of water. Though her mouth had gone bone-dry, she didn't dare drink anything containing caffeine.

"He's in the hospital."

"Oh, no. Is he all right?" She handed Cole and Savannah each a bottle then returned to her seat.

"He's on the mend."

"What happened?"

"Pneumonia." Cole raked a hand through his shaggy hair. "He's been in the hospital for near on a week."

"So he couldn't have killed Rusty."

"Nope."

She wasn't sure why she was so relieved to know that, but of all their suspects, Jim had been the most vulnerable, the most hurt. "We have to let Rhonda know. She'll want to —"

He held up a hand to cut her short. "I've already talked to her. When I found someone who knew Jim, and they told me what had happened, that he'd been taken to the hospital by ambulance, I went to see him. After we spoke, I picked up Rhonda, told her what had happened, and brought her to him. When I left, they were holding hands and crying."

Gia only prayed at least that story had a happy ending.

"What else did Jim say, anything?" Savannah asked.

"He's going to try to get his life back on

track. I told him I'd help him, but the first step is going back home to Rhonda, which he's agreed to do once he's released."

"That's great, Cole. I'm so glad to hear it."

He nodded, and one tear slid down his cheek, then he sniffed and wiped it away. "What about Amanda? Any news?"

They brought him up to speed.

"Good. That's good." He uncapped his water, drank down half the bottle. "I'm glad she'll be okay."

"Me too." While Cole might never come to terms with what had gone on with Amanda and Rusty, at least he could now make amends with Jim. He'd need that, and Gia was so happy he'd have the opportunity.

"Anyway." Cole stood, recapped his water bottle. "Cybil's waiting for me. We're going to make a nice dinner and spend one peaceful evening together away from all of this, so if you ladies are okay?"

"We'll be fine, Cole." Gia stood as well, hugged him tight. "I just have to run up to the apartment — I forgot my charger in the outlet there — and then we're headed out."

"All righty then. I'll see you guys in the morning." He rapped his knuckles against the counter. "Try to shut everything off for a night, and get some rest."

318

"That's exactly what I plan to do."

"Me too," Savannah agreed. "Why don't you go ahead and grab the charger, and I'll finish wrapping the last few bowls and get them put away. Then we can get out of here."

"Sounds good." Gia walked through the café with a smile, careful to lock the door behind her, then unlocked the door to the narrow stairway and jogged up the stairs. She paused in front of the apartment door and sorted through her keys. When she found the right one, she stuffed it into the lock and —

A massive arm wrapped around her from behind and caged her against a rock-hard body. A ham-sized hand clamped over her mouth. "Don't move."

She struggled against his hold. Every self-defense move Hunt had taught her flew right out the window against an attacker so much bigger than her, with an iron grip around her whole body.

"Stop fighting me. I don't want to hurt you."

That makes two of us. But why would he have attacked her from behind if he didn't mean to hurt her? And how had he snuck up on her so quietly. Caleb Ryan hadn't struck her as light on his feet. Fighting

319

against every instinct battering her, Gia worked to relax her body. She stilled, forcing the tension to ease out of her muscles. She begged her brain to slow down, to think. Tremors tore through her. Fear? The waning adrenaline rush?

"Okay. Please. I just want to talk to you."

Then why grab me in a dark hallway? Why not call or knock on the door like a normal person? She nodded.

His hold loosened, and she had to resist the urge to turn and fight or try to escape past him and run down the stairs. When he stepped back from her, she whirled toward him. He held both hands up in front of him. "Please. Just listen to me."

"Okay. But talk fast."

"I know you are engaged to Captain Quinn, so you know things."

She nodded again, unwilling to share any of those things she knew with him.

"The first thing I need to know is if Amanda is okay. I called the hospital, but they won't release any information."

She studied him in the dim light, for the first time noticing the tufts of hair sticking up, the black circles around his eyes, the way his hand shook wildly as he ran it over his goatee. A pang of pity surfaced, but she squashed it back down. "She's out of surgery. The doctors think she's going to make it."

He collapsed against the wall and cupped his face in both hands, deep sobs wracking his body.

Instead of taking the chance to escape, unable to leave anyone in the kind of pain he was clearly suffering with, Gia stood her ground. "Did you shoot her?"

He snapped his head up, met Gia's gaze. "No. No way. I'm in love with her. I'd never do anything to hurt her."

Savannah's theory ran through her head. "Were you the one who killed Rusty?"

"Absolutely not. And before you ask, I don't know who did." He watched her, like a predator sizing up its prey, then let his head fall back against the wall. "But I'm pretty sure Amanda does."

"What? What makes you think that?" And why wouldn't she have told the police if she'd known? Although that information could definitely have gotten her shot.

"Rusty had some shady stuff in his past, and someone found out."

"He was being blackmailed." She ran through the possibilities. They'd already ruled out Jim, since he'd been in the hospital at the time of both attacks. If Caleb was telling the truth, and Rusty was being blackmailed, it made no sense Amanda would have been part of it. Unless Caleb was trying to throw suspicion off himself, which remained a good possibility, it didn't seem likely he was the culprit. So who did that leave? Ariyah? Why? She supposedly loved him, and what would she gain by blackmailing him? Brynleigh? She had been in the forest that morning, and she had accepted a bribe —

"Yeah, he was." Caleb straightened. "And he didn't have enough cash to meet the blackmailer's demands. And Amanda refused to pay. Next thing you know, Rusty received a gift basket filled with muffins, ostensibly from Cole Barrister, with his number and a meeting time on the back of the receipt."

"What did Cole have to do with any of this?"

"Nothing that I know of. I think he was just convenient."

So someone was willing to destroy a man's life just because he was convenient? She wasn't sure she was buying it, but she'd at least hear him out, provided he stayed put against the wall. And if he didn't . . . Well, now that she was face-to-face with him instead of caged against him, a well-aimed kick ought to put him down long enough for her to get past him to the stairs. "You think whoever was blackmailing him decided to kill him and frame Cole?"

He nodded wearily. "I think so."

"Why? Whoever was blackmailing him couldn't collect anything if Rusty was dead."

"Ah, but they could. After Rusty was killed, whoever it was set their sights on Amanda, told her she'd be next if she didn't pay up."

"Was she going to pay?"

"I don't know." He shook his head, ran a hand over his goatee. "I told her to just pay it and be done with the whole thing. But she said if she paid it was simply leaving her open to more extortion later. Then, last night, I wanted to stay with her, but she picked a ridiculous fight and tossed me out. I suspected she planned to meet with the blackmailer this morning, but I was so angry that I ignored my instincts and stormed out anyway. I left her there to get . . ."

"All right. Okay." Gia lay a hand on his wrist. "Why are you telling me all of this?"

"She needs protection. And I need to be there with her. You have to believe me and talk Captain Quinn into providing protection and allowing me to stay with her."

"Why not go to him directly?"

A wry smiled played at the corner of his mouth. "Amanda made me promise I wouldn't go to the police, and I did. I can't go back on my word. I won't. Not to her."

He was splitting hairs as far as Gia was concerned, but if that's what allowed him to live with spilling what he knew, so be it.

"And I also wanted to warn you. Whoever did this is desperate now. They know they're in trouble and they are looking for a way out. If they went after Amanda the way they did, it's possible anyone who's involved might be in danger at this point."

CHAPTER TWENTY-SIX

Hunt checked that the back door was locked, then petted Thor's head. "Are you sure you'll be okay until Savannah gets here?"

"I'll be fine." As she'd assured him about a hundred times already. "Leo took her home to get some things and pick up Pepper, then she's going to spend the night here. We'll be fine."

"All right." He pulled her close, kissed the top of her head. "And there's an officer stationed out front. He'll be there all night, so if you have any problems —"

"I'll just scream." She smiled, but sobered almost instantly. "Do you have someone keeping an eye on Cole and Cybil?"

"Yeah. And Jim and Rhonda too, just in case."

"Did you find Ariyah yet?" She stepped back and looked up at him.

He shook his head, and she could read

the worry in his eyes. "You don't think it was her, though?"

"No."

"But you're afraid she might be a victim?"

"Or she was smart enough to go into hiding." He pursed his lips, scowled. "Either way, I think she knows more than she's admitted."

"What are you going to do about Caleb? Question him further?"

"Yeah, we had two officers take him into custody for attacking you."

She started to bristle, but he held up a hand.

"I know. But we need something to hold him on — it's the only way we can be sure he continues to cooperate and keep an eye on him."

"So, he's at the police station?"

"No. The hospital."

A smile tugged at her. It was good to know at least if Amanda woke up she wouldn't be alone. "Thank you."

"I'm not a total monster, you know."

"So Savannah keeps telling me."

He laughed, the sound warm and comforting. "Just be careful, and I'll let you know if we learn anything new."

"Thank you."

He glanced at his watch. "And now I

really have to go."

"Oh, wait. What about Brynleigh? Do you have someone watching her?"

"We don't have any evidence she's involved in any way, but we are keeping an eye on her."

"Because you want to keep her safe, or because you think she's the killer?"

He shrugged. "Does it matter?"

"I suppose not." Gia walked him to the door, kissed him goodbye, then locked up behind him and turned to Thor and Klondike. "Okay, guys. Savannah told me to pick the movie, so what's it gonna be? Comedy? Romance? Mystery?"

Thor barked once.

Gia laughed. "Okay, then, mystery it is."

She went to the kitchen with Thor and Klondike on her heels, both fully aware there would be some kind of food coming.

Klondike flopped onto a chair, her gaze clinging fiercely to Gia lest Thor get a treat she didn't.

Thor pranced back and forth at Gia's side while she gathered what she'd need for olive oil and rosemary popcorn.

"You know, if the two of you don't stop begging, neither of you will get anything." That was a lie, but she felt the need to at least reprimand them. She pulled out the cast iron pan and set it on the stovetop, then fished her phone from her pocket and set it on the counter next to her. Better to keep it close by. Just in case. "So, what's it gonna be for you two? Chicken or peanut butter?"

Thor stared lovingly, tongue hanging out.

Klondike feigned disinterest.

"Fine. Peanut butter for Thor and catnip for Klondike." She filled Thor's toy with creamy peanut butter, then added catnip to Klondike's ball, and bounced them both across the kitchen. "Go get 'em, guys."

For a moment, she just watched them play, enjoying the feel of being home, the sense of love that filled her house. Then she left them to it and walked into the living room. May as well pick a movie first, give Savannah a little more time before starting the popcorn. She didn't bother sitting down, just picked up the remote, turned on the TV, and started scrolling from where she stood. After the past few days, the last thing she wanted was a nail-biting, edge-of-your-seat action movie. Instead, she settled on a romantic comedy, set it up, and left the remote on the coffee table.

A knock on the door stopped her mid-stride, and she reversed course to open the front door for Savannah. As she reached for the knob, Hunt's repeated warnings blared through her head. Shifting the curtain aside, she peered out the window.

Officer Erickson stood on her front porch, a worried expression on his face.

Hunt. Something must have happened. She ripped the door open, heart in her throat. "Is everything —"

"Step back inside. Quietly, and no one has to get hurt." He whipped a gun from where he'd concealed it behind his leg, shoved through the doorway, and fumbled the lock closed behind him without moving his focus from Gia.

Thor scrambled into the foyer, barking, tail wagging, then skidded to a stop — either at the sight of a stranger or Gia's fear.

Wade shifted the gun toward Thor.

She sidestepped in front of him, caging Thor between her leg and the wall. "No. Stop. Please. He's not going to hurt you. Just let me put him in the kitchen. Please."

He wiped the sweat beading his brow with a sleeve, and gestured toward the back of the house with the weapon.

Gia struggled to move Thor toward the kitchen, his gaze volleying back and forth between her and Wade. Clearly confused, he glued himself to Gia's side, inching back as she did. She prayed he wouldn't attack and get shot, but moving a dog that weighed in at over a hundred pounds and didn't want to be moved was no easy task. Instead of trying to wrestle him back and risk agitating him further, she worked to steady her breathing, slow her heart rate. "He's just confused. If we stand here and converse in normal tones for a few minutes, he'll calm down. You have nothing to fear from him."

The sweat pouring down the sides of his face, soaking his uniform shirt, assured Gia that probably wasn't going to happen. But she had to try. "Please, tell me what's going on. What do you want from me?"

"Money. And information. You give me both of those, and I'll tie you up and leave without hurting anyone." His gaze skittered everywhere, eyeing every corner, every crevice, as if something would jump out from the shadows at any moment and take him down.

If only. Since that wasn't likely to happen, she'd have to rely on her wits. Or just give him what he wanted and let Hunt chase him down afterward. But she needed to do it quickly, before Savannah and Leo showed up and walked into an ambush. "Okay, look. I'm expecting company any minute."

"Sure you are," he sneered.

Maybe better to let him believe that was a lie. She had to think. She maintained a firm grip on Thor's collar as he squirmed.

Wade leveled the gun at her chest, the same height it would have been at when he'd shot Amanda, but right now, there was no one there to save Gia if she went down. Speaking of . . .

"What happened to the police officer outside?"

"He'll live. The last thing I need is to add murdering a police officer to my list of offenses." His hand shook, but he didn't lower the gun. "As long as you give me exactly what I want, I'll disappear and begin a new life somewhere else. No one else has to die, Gia."

That was good to know, especially since she was the one staring down the barrel of his gun. "Okay. Tell me what you want."

"I need money. Cash. I knew I'd eventually have to flee, but I don't have enough saved up to get away, and I'm afraid to touch my hidden accounts just yet. I need to buy myself a little time to get out of the country until the drama dies down." He shrugged a little, his expression tortured. "Really, how long is anyone going to look for Rusty's killer? Guy was a monster. Who really cares what happened to him? Ask me, he got exactly what he deserved."

Clearly, Wade Erickson didn't know Captain Hunter Quinn. He would hunt him to the ends of the earth to get justice for Rusty, for Amanda, for Gia. "Okay, listen. I don't have any cash here."

"None?" he whined.

"Maybe about a few hundred dollars in my purse, but that's it." Who even used cash anymore? Most people paid for nearly everything with a debit card now. Gia wouldn't even have any cash in her bag if not for the fact that she hadn't had time to make it to the bank. "It's yours, and I can give you my debit card too. I'll give you the PIN so you can stop at a cash machine and get as much as you can before leaving town."

Just as long as he left. Maybe Hunt and Leo could trace his movements if he continued to use the card as he fled. Leo! He and Savannah would be there any minute. She had to get Wade out of there before they showed up. "Tell me what information you want."

"I need to know everything the police know. Your boyfriend . . ." He gritted his teeth, swore. "He must suspect me, because he cut me out of the investigation, won't even take my calls."

"Suspect you of what? Killing Rusty?"

"Among other things."

Keep him talking, or get him out as quickly as possible? She couldn't think, needed to give Thor time to calm down. "You were blackmailing him."

He nodded, used his free hand to wipe the back of his neck. "Yeah. But it's not like he didn't deserve it. Bribing Brynleigh like he did. And it's not even like it was the first time. Before I came to Boggy Creek, I worked in law enforcement on the East Coast. Everyone on the force knew Rusty was guilty of bribing officials to get his deals to go through, but no one could prove it. And when I confronted him about it, he just smirked at me. Smirked! With that cocky attitude of his."

He clenched his teeth together, his breathing heavy and erratic as he struggled for control. "I'm sure you can understand I wasn't about to just let that go."

Agitating him further was probably not the smartest idea.

"Anyway, this time I had him cold. And he knew it. Though I will admit, having to remain anonymous when I'd have loved to rub his nose in it . . . Let's just say I bet he wasn't smirking anymore then. He had two choices, pay up or go to jail. But Rusty balked, refused to pay, hunted me down and somehow found out who I was. If he hadn't done that, had just paid his fair share, I never would have had to kill him. It was his own fault. You can't expect me to have left him alive knowing he could point a finger at me as a blackmailer any time he felt like it."

No matter how she'd felt about Rusty, he hadn't deserved to die to protect his blackmailer from being found out. "When he drove into the forest, you were in the passenger seat of his truck."

He nodded. "Captain Quinn tell you that?"

She ignored the question. "But you were on camera entering the forest at four forty-five."

"You think I don't know where those cameras are?" He scoffed. "Please. I went to work, just like I did every other day, then met Rusty at a fire road. I'd planned on framing Jim Kirkman for his murder, but then he went and caused that ruckus at the café, and Cole just landed in my lap. I knew he walked in that area with Cybil, so I lured Rusty out there pretending Cole wanted to meet with him."

"So, why'd he pick you up?"

He laughed, a cold, cruel sound. "To arrest Cole. He knew he could push him into a fight. I was supposed to be his witness, help him destroy the man he hated so much. See what I'm saying? He had me over a barrel, and it would have stayed that way forever if I hadn't gotten rid of him. I'd be like his trained dog. Every time he snapped his fingers, he'd have expected me to come running. Until he eventually tired of the game and turned me in. Which brings me back to Captain Quinn. How much does he suspect?"

Even knowing Rusty had planned on destroying Cole, because she did believe Wade about that, she couldn't condone any of what Wade had done. "I don't think he suspects you. Not that he shares much of his investigations with me, but he didn't mention you at all, and if he was afraid you posed a danger to me, he would have. He probably hadn't called you back because he's been busy."

He studied her, shifted his gaze to Thor for a fraction of a second. Something in his expression set off another round of barking.

Gia did her best to soothe him, keeping her grip on his collar despite the pain in her hand from him trying to break free. "How did you get close to the cop out front?"

"I walked right up to the car, told him Hunt sent me to relieve him, and when he opened the window, I tazed him."

"He's okay, though?"

"Unconscious in the trunk, but he'll be fine."

"Okay, that's good. You haven't gone too far." She started easing backward, fingers twisted in Thor's collar.

He lifted the gun. "Where are you going?"

"To get my bag, so I can give you the cash and card and you can get out of here before anyone else shows up and someone gets hurt needlessly."

"Yeah." He swiped his free hand over his mouth. "Yeah, that'd be good. Let's go."

She herded Thor across the living room toward the kitchen, careful to keep herself positioned between him and the gunman. As she shoved through the door into the kitchen, she spotted Leo peering into the window above the sink. She gestured him back, held her breath and glanced over her shoulder to see if Wade had noticed him.

Wade glanced around the room, his gaze never settling in one place. "Where's the bag?"

She pointed toward the table. Leo's presence changed things. Or did it? Wasn't the main goal still to get Wade out the door? At least now she knew if she could get rid of him, he wouldn't make it far. "It's hanging on the back of the chair."

"Get it."

She hustled Thor toward the table, her hands full of agitated dog. When she reached her bag, she unhooked one handle from the chair and let it fall open, then dug through for the deposit envelope. She pulled it out and tossed it to him without warning. But he caught it with his free hand, gun still level. *Dang.* As she pulled her wallet out, her fingers brushed the canister of bear spray. If she could just get him to lower the gun for a few seconds. She pulled out her wallet and paused. "I'd need two hands to take out the debit card."

"Just give me the wallet." He tucked the deposit envelope into his waistband and held a hand out to her.

She started toward him, wallet held out, and accidentally kicked Klondike's catnip toy and sent it rolling across the tile floor.

Klondike shot from beneath the table after it, straight under Gia's feet.

She stumbled, trying not to land on the tiny cat, and went down hard on one knee, losing her grip on Thor.

Thor lunged before Wade could react and sank his teeth into his arm.

Wade swung the gun around, and Gia scrambled back, yanked her bag off the chair and grabbed the pepper spray. "Thor, stop."

He maintained his hold, shaking his big head back and forth.

Wade fired. Missed. The bullet ricocheted off the floor.

Gia attacked. She put a hand over Thor's eyes, aimed at Wade's face as steadily as she could with her hands shaking, and hit the plunger.

He screamed, stumbled backward.

Thor held on.

"Thor, come." Gia lunged for the gun, had to get it from him. "Let go, Thor."

The door burst open, and Leo shot through. "Freeze! Police. Drop it, Wade."

"Get this dog off me!" he screamed.

Thor clung tight, teeth embedded into his arm, growling deep in his throat.

Wade fired again, the bullet piercing the cabinet beneath the sink.

The next shot tore through Wade's shoulder. As he fell, Thor released his grip and started to pace back and forth in front of him.

Gia fell to her knees and wrapped her arms around his neck, lowered her face into his fur. "It's okay, boy. It's okay. Shhh. Good boy. You're such a good boy."

He stilled as Hunt rushed in and retrieved the gun Wade still clung to. He petted

Thor's head. "Easy, boy. Are both of you okay?"

"Yes. Terrified, but not hurt." Gia buried her head in Thor's side, clinging tightly.

Leaving her and Thor, Hunt handcuffed Wade's hands, in front of him in deference to the wound in his shoulder, then stepped back for the medics to treat him.

"How did you guys know something was wrong?" She smoothed a hand down Thor's side.

"When Leo got here to drop Savannah off, he stopped to check in with the patrol officer and found him missing. We both know Carl. He'd never have left his post. When Leo checked the trunk, he found him unconscious and called it in. Savannah stayed with him while Leo went to check on you."

"Thank you, Leo."

"Any time." He stood over the medic, watching him work on Wade, his jaw firmed.

"The bullet went through his shoulder, doesn't appear to have hit anything major." The medic turned his attention to Wade's arm.

Leo sagged with relief.

Gia couldn't blame him. As angry as she was with Wade for breaking into her home, threatening Thor and her, killing someone then trying to pin it on Cole . . . she wouldn't have wanted him to die at her hand. Or at all. Let him sit in prison where he belonged.

Klondike crept out from beneath a chair, weaved between Gia's knees, rubbed against her ankle.

And Gia sucked in a deep breath, scooped her up, and worked to calm herself down. At least he'd been caught, and Amanda would live. That would have to be enough.

CHAPTER TWENTY-SEVEN

Cole flipped a line of burgers on the grill in Gia's backyard, then tossed one from the platter next to him to Thor.

Thor snatched it from midair.

"Nice catch, boy." Hunt slung his arm around Gia, pulled her tight against his side. "But if you ask me, they should be feeding you a porterhouse."

"Let's not spoil him too much now." Gia petted his head where he stood against her leg. Only a few days had passed since the incident with Wade, and Thor still stuck close. As much as she loved having him at her side, she still felt bad he'd been forced to defend her. Tears threatened.

"Hey." Hunt pulled her even closer, kissed her temple, then twined his fingers with hers on Thor's head. "He's fine, Gia."

She nodded, struggling to regain control of her emotions.

Cole clanged the cowbell beside the grill.

"Come and get it!"

Cole, Cybil, Trevor, Zoe, Alfie, Savannah, Leo, Hunt, and Gia gathered around the picnic table and settled down to eat. Thor lay at Gia's feet.

Leo bent and kissed the top of Gia's head. "I figured you'd want to know Wade Erickson is going to be okay. He had surgery on his arm this morning, and the doctor said he'll be fine."

Gia only nodded, glad to hear Thor hadn't done any permanent damage to him.

He squeezed her shoulder then, opened the cooler and handed out sodas before rounding the table to sit beside Savannah.

Hunt passed her a bowl of coleslaw. "And we spoke to him before he went in, and he made a full confession."

Which made sense. There was no sense denying it when he'd already told Gia everything. But it was a relief to know she wouldn't be called to testify, wouldn't have to relive the moment of terror when Thor lunged at him while he was still armed. Not that she didn't relive it every time she closed her eyes anyway. "And he was working alone? No one else was involved?"

"Seems that way," Hunt said.

"That's good to know."

"And Brynleigh has been relieved of her

position on the zoning commission. The cyber crimes unit is in the process of tracing the payment Amanda made to a secret account of hers. We expect to make an arrest within the week."

Gia filled her plate with coleslaw and potato salad, added a hamburger. "What about Amanda?"

"I feel kind of bad." Savannah lowered her burger to her plate. "I really thought it was her."

Hunt shrugged. "You always have to look at the spouse."

"I guess, but still." She sulked for a minute, then frowned. "What about Ariyah? Does anyone know if she's okay?"

"Yeah, we found her." Leo squeezed her hand. "She won't have to testify, since we already have Wade's confession, but she did witness the murder. She'd followed Rusty into the forest because she didn't believe him that he was meeting up with Cole. She thought he was heading out for a rendezvous with a new lover. She watched Wade shoot him but was too scared to come forward."

Understandable. And Gia could relate because she'd been relieved not to have to testify as well. "But why did she point the finger at Amanda?"

Hunt shrugged. "She saw her in the woods

that morning and thought she had something to do with Rusty's murder. She figured if we picked her up, she'd give up Wade and Ariyah could be kept out of it."

"Are you charging her with anything?"

"Nah." He shook his head. "When we found her, she was terrified, but she eventually did cooperate, so we going to leave her be."

"Any word on Amanda?"

"Caleb has been at her bedside since her surgery. Apparently, he'd been in the forest that day to keep an eye on her. The two of them are planning to get married. And apparently, they're going to be your new neighbors. They're planning to relocate to Boggy Creek and open the bakery."

Gia laughed. She only hoped Caleb's attitude would improve before they opened. "Okay, enough talk of murder. There has to be something else going on in Boggy Creek."

"Not yet." Trevor clapped his hands and rubbed them together. "But a little birdie told me Savannah and I are about to get to work planning a wedding."

ABOUT THE AUTHOR

Lena Gregory is the author of the Bay Island Psychic Mystery series, which takes place on a small island between the north and south forks of Long Island, New York, and the All-Day Breakfast Café Mystery series, which is set on the outskirts of Florida's Ocala National Forest.

Lena Grew up in a small town on the south shore of eastern Long Island, where she still lives with her husband, three kids, son-in-law, and five dogs, and works full-time as a writer and freelance editor.

To learn more about Lena and her latest writing endeavors, visit her website at www.lenagregory.com/, and be sure to sign up for her newsletter at lenagregory.us12.list -manage.com/subscribe?u=9765d0711ed 4fab4fa31b16ac&id=49d42335d1.

The employees of Thorndike Press hope you have enjoyed this Large Print book. All our Thorndike Large Print titles are designed for easy reading, and all our books are made to last. Other Thorndike Press Large Print books are available at your library, through selected bookstores, or directly from us.

For information about titles, please call:
   (800) 223-1244

or visit our website at:
   gale.com/thorndike

Printed in the USA
CPSIA information can be obtained
at www.ICGtesting.com
JSHW020157290924
70552JS00005B/5